HEIRESS UNDONE

PACIFIC PASSIONS - BOOK THREE

COURTNEY CLARK MICHAELS

AUGUST PUBLISHING

For my husband.
Ou te alofa ia te oe.

CONTENT NOTES

This book contains the depiction of PTSD, on-page panic attack, adoption as a main theme.

Every effort has been made by the author to handle this content with sensitivity, however please prioritise your self-care.

GLOSSARY

Aiga – family
Talofa lava – hello (formal)
Malo – Hello (informal)
Lo'u pepe – my baby
Fale – house
Puletasi – a traditional style of modest two-piece dress worn in the Pacific Islands
Lavalava – a traditional item of clothing worn by men and women in the Pacific Islands, similar to a wraparound skirt or a sarong
Itiiti tuafafine - little sister
Fafine aulelei - beautiful woman

PROLOGUE

Oliana Maiava was dying.

A tight band wound its way across her midsection, pressing against her lungs, constricting her airflow. Sweat beaded under her arms, thankfully hidden by the demure sleeves of her dress. Around her, members of her family, her *aiga*, chatted and laughed, buoyed by good food, good music and the good grace of being together in the days before Christmas. If they looked at her a little longer, a little more closely, well that was to be expected. She had been announced as the secret princess of Avali mere hours ago.

Is this how I go? A heart attack in the middle of a family reunion while they all gossip about my true parentage? Oliana sucked in another shallow lungful of air. Gods, that would be just her luck. To go toes up under the scrutiny of her entire *aiga*. The only person not shooting her inquisitive looks, in fact, was her biological father. King Tama, the man she'd thought was her uncle until three months ago, was just *there*, his ubiquitous assistant Iosefa flanking him. Her imminent demise would probably be a relief to the king - he'd barely spoken to her in the weeks since she'd discovered he'd adopted her out to his sister-in-law and her husband at birth. If not for Prince Aleki and Prince Manu discovering the truth, she might never have known.

Which might have been a blessing...

Ostensibly, this pre-Christmas family reunion was a reception for Prince Aleki and his wife Stella, who'd broken royal protocol and more than a few hearts when they had married in secret earlier in the year. But the announcement of her royal status had changed all that. Oliana was most definitely the centre of attention and the knowledge crawled up her throat in waves of sticky discomfort.

Even knowing the announcement was coming, even with the weeks she'd had to come to terms with the news and the decades of lies of her adoptive parents, nothing could have prepared her for the feeling of being stripped bare by the eyes of her family. And found wanting.

"You look like you're thinking glum thoughts." Oliana's recently-discovered brother Manu's fiancée, Clare, flopped into the seat beside her, her grin peeping over her cocktail glass.

"Alcohol is the devil's juice," Oliana responded primly, the words of her youth flowing from her lips without hesitation. She turned back towards the party.

"Ain't that the truth. You want some?" Oliana shot a look at the curvy, dark haired woman, who waggled her eyebrows and her glass in unison. Clare had only arrived on the island last week for the first time but the feisty scientist had made quite an impact. Oliana's parents -*adoptive parents* - had had a lot to say about Manu's choice of wife and none of it positive.

That was enough to make up her mind. She held out a hand and Clare deposited the glass in it. Oliana took a quick sip, the burn of alcohol balanced by the icy tang of the mixer and the sweetness of lime.

"What is it?"

"A London Mule. Gin based. You know, the liquor of colonisers."

Oliana shot Clare a quick look as she handed the glass back. Avali had managed to fight off the waves of British colonists sent to the Pacific until the only thing that remained was their religion, which Avalians had taken up with a vengeance.

"Interesting choice," she muttered under her breath, and Clare beamed at her.

"It is, isn't it? The way I figure it, some of the people here are going to be pissed anyway because Stella and I are *palagi* and we've wrangled your hot princes. Between Stella's secret wedding and my job undoing all of God's will regarding infertility, there's not much we can do if people are determined to dislike us. I might as well drink what I want." She sucked down another long swallow of her cocktail and handed the glass back to Oliana.

She drank again, the liquor mixing with the heat in her chest, the increased pace of her breath. Clare's words brought back the expectations of her adoptive parents as they'd prepared for her debut tonight.

'You're the last chance at keeping the royal bloodline one hundred percent Avalian.'

The thought weighed on her, pressing down on her shoulders and on the ever-shrinking hope that she might one day be able to live her own life. For twenty four years she'd been at the mercy of her parents and their demands. To be the perfect daughter, to be humble, kind and modest. She'd enrolled in university as a Psychology major after high school, only to drop out before classes started because of her father's derision and her mother's disappointment. Instead, she'd let them push her into teaching kindergarten and volunteering.

Hindsight is twenty-twenty. Obviously, they'd known this time would come, when Oliana would learn the truth about her heritage and need the skills required to survive as Pacific royalty, but it still stung. She'd been forced into tiny boxes her whole life and if the assessing looks her family - the people who were supposed to support her - were aiming her way was any indication, it was only going to get worse when the media and general public learned about her.

"This is it." Desolation pushed the words out of her chest into the sea-scented air of the marquee.

"What is what?" Clare took back her drink.

Outside on the lawn the band stopped playing and a man's voice rang out through the speaker, but Oliana ignored it.

"My life. I'm never going to be able to be anything else. Princess Oliana. That's all I am now."

Her future sister-in-law frowned. "I don't think that's true. Look at Manu. He still gets to play sports. He has a real job as well as being a royal."

Oliana shook her head. "It's not the same. You couldn't understand." Clare had been raised in New Zealand and was unfamiliar with Avalian culture and customs.

"It's different for Manu because he's a man. The same way Avalian sons can go out with their friends but daughters require chaperones."

The traditional beliefs hadn't bothered Oliana before, but the pressure rising now under her skin threatened to explode as all the things she'd never get a chance to do ran through her mind, slide by slide, like a film filled with sound and colour and joy. Experiences that were miles from the life she'd already lived, and from the staid future that awaited her as the sole Avalian princess.

Clare leaned forward and touched her arm, but before she could speak a panicked shout echoed through the marquee.

"Call a doctor!"

A hush ran through the crowd and in the quiet that followed, a female voice spoke in English.

"Calm down, Aleki. My water broke, it's not a national emergency."

Through the press of bodies, Oliana caught a glimpse of her oldest cousin-*brother*-stalking across the wooden dance floor, pushing his pregnant wife in a wheelchair. Manu walked behind him, his phone to his ear as he scanned the room frantically.

"Oh shit," Clare muttered, and stood, hustling towards her fiancé, whose eyes lightened in relief when he saw her.

A pang of worry echoed through Oliana. Stella wasn't due until early February according to Aleki, who had mentioned it at one of the weekly meetings they'd been holding to prepare her for royal duties. But as the noise from the crowd grew and onlookers swarmed towards the entrance of the marquee, Oliana's concern for Stella faded into blissful awareness that for the first time in a very, very long time, nobody was looking at her.

So she did the one thing her body had been screaming at her to do for weeks.

She ran.

ONE

Ninety-eight, ninety-nine, one hundred.

Theo Miller finished his last sit-up and rolled over, beads of sweat dripping from his forehead to the polished wooden floorboards of his London flat despite the late December chill that seeped in through the open window. Palms flat against the floor, he lifted his body up and lowered it to an inch from the ground again. *One, two, three...*

His phone rang, but he let it go to voicemail. Reaching one hundred push-ups, he stood and repeated the same number of squats.

One hundred sit-ups. One hundred push-ups. One hundred squats. Three times a day.

The routine had been part of his life since his teens, shoved into foster care full of rage without an outlet. As he'd grown, he'd added running and the gym to his repertoire, but the pattern relaxed him, knowing that he could do it wherever he was, at any time he chose. He needed it more and more at the moment, as the nightmares that plagued his sleeping hours left him tense and restless when dawn came.

Finishing up, he checked his phone and immediately dialled the number he'd missed a call from.

"Hello?"

"Hey hey, Clarity Sage." Theo settled back on his bed, the plain grey coverlet cool against his back. "How's your island Christmas going?" His former foster sister and best friend was spending the holidays on the tropical Pacific island of Avali with her fiancé, one of the nation's princes.

"Not great," Clare sighed. "We've lost a princess."

Theo arched an eyebrow, despite the fact she couldn't see him. "Did you check the stables? A nearby meadow? Where do princesses hang out these days?"

"Don't be a smart arse," Clare snapped, her irritation clear over their connection and he grinned, the familiarity of their exchange a warm balm. "She took a plane, like all good runaways."

"How long ago?"

"Six days."

"Clare, we spoke at Christmas. That was four days ago. Why did you not mention it then?"

"We, uh, didn't know about it then."

Theo let his silence speak for him, and she sighed. "I know. There was a lot going on here. Stella's early labour, the baby, the press interest. It was all a bit of a mess. Both sides of the family seemed to think she was with the other, and today we realised that nobody had actually seen her since the family reunion."

"Jesus, what is their security like?" Theo breathed, professional judgement pushing its way to the front.

Clare groaned. "I knew you'd say that. Pacific Island royalty isn't like British royalty. They don't have bodyguards and shit."

"Alright," he said, already moving towards the spare

room of his flat where his computers were set up. "What do you need from me then?"

"Can you find her? Airport footage has her leaving on a plane to Sydney early on Christmas Eve, and continuing on to London. The boys are going crazy not knowing where she is. She's never left Avali before by all accounts."

"I can try." Theo took down the details he needed - Oliana Maiava, a birth date that made her barely twenty four, her tax and health numbers in the Avalian system and her cellphone number, as well as the details of her flight to Australia.

"This could take a while," he warned Clare as he booted up his systems. "I'll let you know as soon as I have something."

"Thanks, Tex. Love you."

His blood ran cold. *Tex, Tex, Tex.* The hated nickname reverberated in his head and he had to work to force words past the sudden lump in his throat.

"Love you too, Clare Bear." He hung up and tossed his cellphone on the desk beside him.

His skin crawled, clammy and cold, with the memories the name invoked. Clare might have started calling him that, but after more than a decade hearing it from his Army buddies, it brought back nothing but bad memories. Pulling on a cardigan that had been slung over the back of his computer chair to ward off the chill of his bare torso, he opened the first programme.

Should I call Liam? The thought bounced into his head and he dismissed it quickly. Liam was the other partner in their fledgling cybersecurity firm, Spire Security, also military-trained, out of Britain's National Cyber Force to Theo's New Zealand Army. He dismissed the thought quickly. Liam was spending the holidays with his family in

Dorset, and didn't need Theo calling him about a mate's missing sister-in-law. In the end, it didn't take as long as he'd thought to find Oliana Maiava. She might be runaway royalty, but she sure as hell wasn't trying to hide. He rang Clare's number again.

"Hello?"

"Found her."

"It's only been a couple of hours."

A reluctant grin pulled at the corners of his mouth. Clare might call him a genius, despite the fact that the girl could literally create human life in a lab, but her grasp on his work was tenuous at best. "Yes."

"Hang on then, let me get the others." A scuffle on the other end of the phone, a slammed door, and she spoke into the phone again. "Switching you to video."

He propped his phone on the tripod he kept on his desk for such occasions in time to see Clare's face pop up on screen. Two hulking Pacific Islanders sat on either side of the petite brunette, her fiancé Manu and his brother Aleki, the heir to Avali. Behind them, Aleki's wife Stella stood, cradling a baby to her chest.

"Hi everyone." He'd met Clare's future in-laws before at one of Manu's rugby league games and was surprised at how down-to-earth the royals were.

Manu and Stella greeted him warmly, and Aleki nodded, moving straight to the point. "You have found Oliana?"

"Yup. She's here in London."

Two sets of dark eyebrows shot high on brown foreheads at his words. "London?" Aleki croaked. "I assumed that would be a stopover. What is she doing in London?"

"No idea," Theo shrugged. "Her phone records don't show contact with anyone in the city from before she left, but she arrived early on Christmas morning on a flight from Sydney that stopped over in Dubai. She stayed at a hostel in Brixton for the first two nights and her location is currently Muswell Hill, in North London."

"Right." Aleki's tone was decisive. "Well, you can go collect her and bring her back then."

Theo felt his own eyebrows climb. "Interesting idea. I'm not actually in the human trafficking business though. She's here of her own accord because she wants to be. I'm not going to force her back to a country she fled from under the cover of night."

"Of course not," Stella soothed in the background. "That would be lunacy. And extremely high handed." She gave her husband a hard look.

Manu stroked his chin. "What about reconnaissance?"

"What about it?" Theo asked.

"Well," Manu continued. "She must be there for a reason. We don't know what that reason is, but we want to make sure she's safe. You could keep an eye on her, make sure she's protected, that she's not at risk."

"I have a job, you know," Theo offered mildly. "Have any of you tried simply talking to her?"

"Our cousin Sio did." Aleki looked miserable. "He called her this morning when we realised she was missing. She asked him if he'd known she was adopted and when he said he'd always suspected she told him to fuck off and die."

"I love her," Clare breathed in awe, the sound coming through Theo's headphones in a rush of air.

Manu glared at his fiancée who twinkled back at him and Theo tried to hide the delight that poured through his body. Seeing Clare so happy, engaged to a man she *twinkled* at for God's sake, was all he'd ever wanted for her. He was thrilled she'd found joy.

"So about your job." Aleki's voice cut through the headphones. "You work in security, yes?"

"Cybersecurity, yes."

"But you have military training?"

"I do." Theo lingered over the words, unsure of where this was going.

"In that case, I would like to hire you to watch over Oliana while she is in the United Kingdom. Make sure she is safe, and report back to us if there are any concerns. We'll give it a week until we approach her again, maybe give her a chance to cool off." The eldest prince grimaced. "This has been a difficult transition for her, and perhaps all she wants is a holiday. But we need to ensure her safety. She has never been off the island before. She doesn't have the experience to avoid pickpockets or other risks. And of course there are the paparazzi. The British media can be ruthless. You're on the ground there, you know the area and you're not someone she would connect to Avali."

"I'm also not a bodyguard," Theo reminded him.

"That is of no matter," Aleki waved a hand. "Manu is right. You are merely providing reconnaissance. We will pay you handsomely." He named a figure that made Theo's pulse leap.

"For the whole time?"

"Per week," Aleki replied, and Theo tried not to let his excitement show. Liam came from money, but Theo had had to sell his flat in Auckland for the start-up costs for the business. More importantly, the opportunity to secure a contract with a royal family would be a huge step towards their goal of working with high profile individuals and families. The goal they'd come up with one night in a dive bar in Kandahar over a few too many beers after a hard day of trying to fell a regime and forget the impact their drone strikes made on the city's civilians. The goal they'd been working towards ever since the morning after when they'd woken up with mild hangovers and the clear realisation that they'd both rather be doing anything but watching people die on tiny screens for the rest of their lives. This was it. This was the breakthrough they'd been waiting for. Liam's contacts were great, but they weren't foreign royalty. A contract with the Esera family would set them up for the kind of long-term success they'd only dreamt about.

"Okay," he said. "I'll send over a contract in an hour. If the terms are to your liking, I'll do it. I'll surveil your sister while she's here."

"THERE'S A MAN STARING AT ME," Oliana whispered to her boss.

"I'm not surprised," Gert responded loudly, her North London accent booming through the small bookshop. "You're not bad looking, you know. Enjoy it. One day you'll be as old as me and they won't look any more. You'll miss it then."

Ana watched as the slight, dark-haired man shot them another look and scurried out of the door, the shop bell ringing behind him.

"That wasn't nice," she told Gert, who cackled away merrily from where she sat on the stairs that led to the apartment above. "Ah, you've got to test their mettle early, love. If he couldn't handle that, what good would he be in the long run?"

Ana smiled and straightened the display of glittery pens by the register. It was only her second day at the shop, but already she knew that working with Gert would give her more life experience than almost a quarter of a century on Avali had. She'd been one of a dozen applicants to answer the online ad for a studio flat above the small bookshop in Muswell Hill, according to Gert, but the only one not already gainfully employed, and the older woman wasn't fool enough—in her words— to turn down a tenant and an employee in one package. And she wasn't too fussed about a working visa either, she'd added. The very act of having a job sent a thrill down Ana's spine. She'd had paid employment before, but her part-time job at the preschool always seemed like a ploy on her parents' part to make her seem like good wife material, and she'd been expected to contribute her whole paycheck to the family account. It was an okay job, but the idea of earning her own money, of being able to buy what she wanted without asking for approval was heady. And she needed the money too. She'd cleared out her savings account on her way out of Avali. Twenty-four years worth of birthday money, Christmas money and any accrued interest, which it turned out had been just enough to cover flights, two weeks rent upfront on her tiny flat, and the luxury of a haircut. Her waist length mane was gone, cut to a thick mass that brushed her collarbones. No more buns, no more braids - the new length wouldn't allow for it, and a surge of triumph passed through her at the knowledge that when she went back to Avali, there was one part of her rebellion she'd be able to take with her.

The shop bell jangled again and she looked up from the pens.

Oh. Now him, she wouldn't mind staring at her.

The man who'd wandered in wouldn't have been out of place on one of the covers of the romance novels that lined the back shelves. He was huge, at least six four and at six foot herself, Ana considered herself well placed to judge.

Late twenties, early thirties maybe. Massive shoulders, long legs, short blond hair and stubble that covered a jawline that could cut diamonds. He looked over towards her, the skin around his hazel eyes crinkled and she about came on the spot.

"Jesus, Mary and Joseph," Gert muttered behind her. "Now that's a man."

He approached the desk.

"Hello, ladies." Not British, then. An Australian or Kiwi maybe? She didn't have a lot of experience with accents to draw on, but he sounded like a male version of Aleki and Manu's partners. The thought of her cousins - her brothers - sobered her. She hadn't quite wrapped her brain around the fact that the cousins she'd grown up with were her blood brothers, or what that meant for her relationship with her adopted brother Sio.

"Can I help you?" She managed the question around the betrayal that squeezed her throat, and the heaviness of her heart must have sounded in her voice because he cocked his head and studied her for a second

"I'm looking for a diary," he said finally. "New year ahead and all that."

"Sure," she nodded. "Over there by the window." She pointed and his gaze followed her arm to the wall where the planners and stationery items sat bathed in a weak shaft of London's winter sun.

"Cheers," he said, and sauntered over to the display, giving Ana a glorious view of the long line of his back beneath the thick charcoal wool of his peacoat.

Gert made her way to the counter and peered over at the customer. "Would you get a load of that backside?"

"I don't think we're supposed to objectify the customers, Gert," Ana replied primly.

"It's my shop, love. I'll do what I want." Gert waggled her brows over rheumy eyes and Ana bit back a smile. "Ooh, look, he's bending down."

Ana snuck a glance over towards the display where he had indeed crouched down to examine products on the lowest shelf. His coat rose up as he bent forward, and she caught a glimpse of a truly magnificent backside under worn denim.

"What a waste," Gert sighed mournfully. "Were I but fifty again, I'd make him my own." She elbowed Ana, who flinched. Gert might look like a sweet little old octogenarian in her floral skirt and woollen sweater, but her elbows were as razor-sharp as her wit. "Have a go then, love. He doesn't have a ring on."

"I'm not interested in men," Ana lied loftily.

"You a lesbian then?" Gert squinted at her. "You should have said something. Janice down at the bakery has a nice bisexual niece I can set you up with."

"No!" Ana said, heat rising in her face. "I mean, I'm interested in men, I'm just not interested in dating. I don't think." Flames fanned her cheeks as her thoughts turned to the blue and white striped notebook on the tiny bedside table in her apartment. She'd seen it on the shelf yesterday and handed over one of her last ten pound notes to Gert on the spot. Last night she'd sat at the dinette, opened it to the first gloriously blank page and in a smooth black ink carefully copied down the list she'd jotted down on an airplane napkin on her flight from Sydney. The list of things she wanted to achieve with this trip - her lifelong ambitions, all crowded down to be shoved into one short burst of freedom before the walls of island royalty closed on her forever.

1.Cut hair. She'd already done it by the time the note-book arrived in her life, but she'd written it down anyway, relishing in the ability to tick it off immediately in the pink pen she'd borrowed from down by the cash register especially for that purpose.

2. *Stay out all night.*
3. *Attend a protest.*
4. *Go skinny dipping.*
5. *Get a tattoo.*
6. *Lose virginity.*

IT WAS number six that haunted her thoughts now. It wasn't that she thought it was that big of a deal, she was still going to be *her*, whether she'd had a penis in her or not; and years of horse riding had pretty much shattered any chance that her hymen might still be intact. But it was the only one she couldn't do by herself. Certainly, she could pay a professional to help her with it, like she had with her haircut and would for the tattoo, but that seemed a bit clinical. The entire reason for her escape was to live life like a normal twenty-four year old woman, and she was reasonably sure that most twenty-four year old women didn't hire escorts, if only for the additional expense to their stretched Gen Z budgets.

Capitalism foils us again.

But first, she needed a man to help her. So when the customer returned to the counter holding a burgundy leather diary, she smiled. Brightly. Too brightly, maybe, because his light brown eyebrows lifted. She dialled it down.

"Did you find everything you were looking for?"

"Yup." He placed the diary on the counter and shoved his hands into his pockets, rocking back on his heels, eyes steady on her.

"Is there anything else you'd like today?"

His hazel eyes warmed. "What would you recommend?"

Ana gathered her breath. *Don't panic. You can do this.*

"I'd recommend the pasta at Rafaella's. Would you like to get dinner sometime?"

A slow smile spread across his face, confident and easy.

"I'd love to. Does tonight suit?"

Oh my gosh, oh my gosh, oh my gosh. She wrestled her inner voice down and smiled sweetly at him.

"I'm free tonight. I'll meet you there at seven."

"Seven it is." He held out his hand. "I'm Theo."

She shook it, hoping he couldn't feel the trembling in her fingers. She'd done it. She'd asked someone out. And he'd accepted! "I'm Ana." She'd used the nickname one of the girls she volunteered with called her when applying for the flat and it felt good. Oliana was a Pacific princess, with a messy family and a list of responsibilities that wore on her like sandpaper. Ana lived in London above a bookshop and asked good looking men on dates.

"Ana." He repeated the word, rolling it over his tongue in his antipodean accent, the vowels stretching and lingering in the space between them. "I'll see you then."

The bell rang as he exited, and Ana grasped the counter, breathing deeply in through her nose.

"Well done, love. I'm impressed." Through her inhalations, she caught the respect in Gert's tone and her heart leapt in pride. She could do this. She could be bold and brave in a way that even Gert, with her acerbic nature, could appreciate. "The pasta at Rafaella's is crap, though, to be honest."

Ana burst out laughing.

TWO

Gods, it's freezing.

Ana stomped her way down the icy footpath, head down, arms wrapped around herself to ward off the worst of the wind's bite. She'd packed her warmest clothes when she'd left Avali, but the island's coldest days had nothing on the bitter chill of a London winter. Gert had tossed a couple of long sleeved tops bearing the bookstore's logo at her when she'd been hired and between those and the store's heating system, she was managing at work, but the night air was a different beast. She'd popped out to the charity shop down the road on her break and bought a plain black coat but you got what you paid for, and she hadn't paid much.

"Ana?"

She looked up. Ah, so she hadn't imagined it then. He was beautiful. Like if Michaelangelo's David had a baby with a Hemsworth and raised it with the skincare routine of Paul Rudd. He stood in a golden pool of light in front of Rafaella's, his back against the plate glass window, breath misting in the air.

"Hi," she croaked.

"Hi," he replied.

Say something else! You're just staring at him! She ignored the voice in her head, drinking in the sight of him in his charcoal coat and black trousers, the buzzing in her ears growing louder the longer they looked at each other, a gorgeous white noise that drowned out the traffic on Muswell Hill Broadway and softened the edges of her vision.

"Shall we?" Theo asked finally, tipping his head towards the restaurant. Relief filtered into her veins because at least one of them still had their senses about them.

"Certainly."

He held the door for her and her chair as they were seated. Had she heard him swallow when she shrugged off her coat? She couldn't be sure. She'd done the best she could with short notice and a meagre selection, choosing a plain black sweater that hugged her curves, a flippy red skirt, black tights and low ankle boots.

Theo slung his own coat over the back of his chair, and tilted it so that when he sat his back was to the wall. He scanned the room quickly and smiled at her over the burnished glow of the little tealight candle between them before flipping open his menu.

"You said the pasta's good?"

Discomfort prickled over her skin. "I don't actually know," she admitted. "I only moved into the neighbourhood three days ago. It was the first place that came to mind when I was talking to you."

Theo looked up from his menu, a slow smile spreading across his face. Even his teeth were perfect.

"Yeah?"

"Yes." Ana straightened her spine, determined to brazen it out. This was what she'd come here for. A chance to be herself, free from the limitations of the little box her adoptive parents had tried to force her into her whole life. She wanted to be the kind of woman who asked men out, who kissed them on darkened streets and maybe went home with them. And it was now or never. The crown hung over her head like the sword of Damocles, constantly niggling in the back of her mind. A month, max. That's all the time she could reasonably expect before her family figured out where she was and arrived to drag her back to a sheltered life of constant responsibilities and expectations.

"Well," he said, hazel eyes twinkling. "Let's see what Rafaella's has to offer us."

The waitress came and Ana ordered a London Mule without looking at the drinks list, since it was the only cocktail she knew the name of. Theo ordered sparkling water and she tried not to judge him for it, but honestly didn't he think it tasted like carbon and sadness?

"So," he said, after the waitress had left with a promise to be back with their drinks shortly. "You've just moved up to Muswell Hill? Where were you before?"

"Brixton," she replied. Sure, she'd only been there two days, but it seemed a bit early in the relationship to reveal that she'd run away from a tropical island nation she might in fact be the missing princess of. Their bread basket hadn't even arrived.

"Where do you live?"

"Clapham."

"Is that near here?"

The corners of his eyes crinkled again in a way that made her stomach swoop, and she dragged her gaze from his, fiddling with her silverware so she wouldn't throw herself bodily at him in the middle of a mid-range Italian eatery. "No, miles away actually," he replied.

"Oh? What were you doing up here this morning?"

"I had to meet someone for business."

"What do you do?"

"I'm in IT."

Ana nearly laughed out loud, but caught herself at the last moment, schooling her features into the neutrally polite expression she wore at church and with her parents' friends. He had the body of a professional wrestler and a face to rival Hollywood royalty, and he spent his time messing about with computers in windowless rooms? Admittedly, her actual experience with IT technicians was low, but the media always seemed to portray them as pasty-skinned men, surviving entirely on a diet of Mountain Dew and incel ideology.

"That sounds fantastically boring," she offered honestly, and he threw his head back and laughed, the long column of his throat working. She wanted to lick it.

"It can be," he confirmed once he'd recovered. "But I enjoy it. I love finding problems and working out solutions. Plus every so often a job comes along that takes you by surprise. Who doesn't love surprises?" His smile was wicked now, and Ana felt a stirring low in her torso in response.

She was saved from having to answer by the waitress, who deposited their drinks and took their order. Careful to heed Gert's warning, Ana avoided the pasta in favour of veal medallions in a masala sauce, and Theo ordered the pumpkin and blue cheese risotto.

"Are you a vegetarian?" Ana asked, when they'd been left alone again, and he nodded, lifting his glass of revolting sparkling water to his lips for a sip.

"Pescatarian. I don't like meat," he offered, when he'd lowered the offending glass to the table again. "The look of it, the smell. It brings up things I'd rather forget."

"Do you want me to change my order?" Ana asked, a little bubble of anxiety weaving its way up her chest. "I don't want to make you uncomfortable."

He waved away her suggestion. "No, no, nothing like that. It doesn't bother me when others eat it. It's just not for me."

"I had a friend like that once," she confided. "Where I come from, it's very unusual to be a vegetarian. And she refused, right from the time she was little. Which would have been fine, I suppose, but her parents owned a pig farm. All free range, all organic, but there were a lot of peanut butter sandwiches in her life before she was old enough to cook her own dinners."

"Where are you from?" he asked lightly, his eyes searching hers, and the anxiety in her chest spread, crawling up her throat. She didn't want to lie to him, this sweet, interesting guy, but she couldn't risk him looking up Avali either. The chances of her disappearance being reported would be high by now, unless the royal family was covering it up. The same way King Tama had covered up her very existence for years.

"The South Pacific," she answered. He cocked a brow and she rushed to cover her evasiveness with another question. "You?"

"The South Pacific," he responded, and when she frowned at him, he smiled back. "I'm from New Zealand. I lived in Dunedin when I was young and then moved up to Auckland. My last job brought me to London and I've been here for about six months now."

Ana felt her shoulder unclench at the additional details he offered and hated herself for her hypocrisy.

"Do you like London?" she asked, as the waitress arrived with two steaming plates of food, and she moved back in her chair to allow the other girl room to set the plates down.

"I do," he confirmed. "I've travelled a bit and I like the way London manages to feel like a lot of small towns mashed into one big city. Plus it's great for work. There are a lot of people here who can use the services I provide." His eyes stayed on her as she cut her veal. He waited until she'd placed a forkful in her mouth before asking, "What about you? Why are you in London, Ana?"

SHE TOOK IT WELL, her eyes widening slightly and she gestured at her full mouth to indicate she needed a minute, but he could practically see the gears turning in her head. He was in over his own head already. Today's recon at the bookshop should have been enough, but she'd gone and thrown a spanner in the works by asking him out, and even if she wasn't an absolute stunner with almond-shaped brown eyes, thick dark hair and long tanned limbs that went on for days, he was hardly going to turn her down. He'd get a lot more information by going to dinner with her than he ever would by becoming instantly recognisable as the guy who'd turned her down.

"I, um," she lifted her drink to her lips and took a long swallow. Procrastinating. "I'm here for a month or so. On a working holiday." The princess of Avali smiled weakly at him over her cocktail and his dick stirred in his pants. He didn't love the fact that she was lying directly to his face, but damn if she wasn't cute all the same. Not that it mattered. She was a job, and beyond that, Manu's sister. He liked Clare's new fiancé. He didn't want the rugby league player stabbing him to death in the night because he'd had impure thoughts about one of his siblings. And she was definitely the Esera-Maiava sibling to inspire them. Theo swung both ways, but Aleki was as uptight as they came, while Ana was a genuine delight. Funny, brash and so pretty to look at he felt like he was falling when she flashed the dimple in her left cheek at him.

"What are you planning to do while you're here?" Perhaps she did have a plan, contacts, something she was trying to accomplish that might be dangerous for Avali.

A pink flush crept up her neck and she studied her veal intently. "I have a list of things I'd like to do."

"The London Eye? The Tower?"

She shook her head slightly. "Those would be nice, but this is more of a personal list. Things I've always wanted to do but haven't been able to do at home."

Bingo. Not a senseless runaway, she was here on a mission. Theo leaned closer, reaching out to cover one of her hands with his. Her brown skin was warm, and his skin tingled at the contact, soaking up the heat and letting it sink into his bones.

"That sounds exciting." He took a deep breath and plunged in. "Do you have family here?"

Her face shuttered immediately. It was impressive. "No." She reached for her cocktail, seemed to realise she'd drained it during his last question and picked up her water glass instead. Avoiding his eyes, she took a long drink. He'd be able to report back to Aleki and Manu that their sister seemed well-hydrated, if nothing else.

"Are they excited to hear about your travels?"

"I doubt it." She was shovelling food in now, her cutlery flashing in the low candlelight like warning lights.

"How about-"

"Tell me about your family," she interrupted, and he hid

a smile behind his own waterglass at her attempted deflection.

"I don't have much of one," he offered truthfully. Maybe if he offered up his own messy, scarred background, she'd be more inclined to give up her own details. "My last surviving family member died when I was thirteen. I spent some time in foster care, and was adopted when I was fifteen by a nice older couple that I see every now and then."

"You only see your adoptive parents every now and then?" Her gaze was curious, and he remembered that up until a couple of months ago she hadn't even known the people who'd raised her were anything other than her birth mother and father.

"I think adoption can be a tricky subject," he offered carefully. "I was almost a legal adult when I was adopted and I joined the army as soon as I finished school. The Millers were very welcoming. They gave me their last name and provided me with a place to live, food, everything I had wanted growing up, but in a lot of ways they still feel like strangers. I visit when I'm back in New Zealand, but for most of my life growing up, I was on my own. I think I prefer it like that."

"I was never alone growing up," Ana blurted. She looked as surprised as he was that she'd said it.

"No?"

"No," she shook her head. "Girls in the Pacific aren't really allowed out much by themselves. There was always my brother with me, or one of my cousins." Discomfort danced across her face, drawing her dark brows inwards.

"Did that bother you?"

"Sometimes. More, now that I think back on it. I never did anything wrong, never said I was going somewhere and went somewhere else. I followed all the rules, all the time. There was no need for me to be watched that carefully. I didn't go anywhere by myself until I was twenty, until I was a legal adult. I used to get up early and swim in the ocean." A sweet smile lit her face. "That was my alone time."

"Did you want more?" Theo asked, and her smile flatlined.

"Yes. I always wanted more."

"What does more look like to you?" Theo pressed, and her lips rolled together in a grim line.

"Something different. Something I can't get on the island."

Still no specifics.

"Anything in particular?"

"A date who doesn't interrogate me might be nice."

Theo forced himself further back into his seat, letting the tension drain out of his shoulders, throwing out an easy chuckle.

"Sorry, sweetheart. You'll have to forgive my interest. It's been a long time since I found a woman as fascinating as you."

Her gaze was blatantly suspicious, but she nodded once. The electric charge in his fingertips quieted. He'd been too eager, too keen for any additional information he could offer up in his report to the Avalian princes. Technically, he wasn't even supposed to be talking to her, just watching, but the opportunity had presented itself and here he was, mining her for facts to bolster his own career prospects, to prove he was good enough to work with the upper echelon. Theo was self-aware enough to see his own flaws, but the fact that he couldn't keep his shit together enough to keep a smile on Ana's round face for the length of a single date indicated that he needed to cool his jets.

"You said you're not particularly interested in the tourist attractions, but you should definitely consider checking out some of the museums while you're here," he offered, and they moved into a polite conversation about different exhibits that were available around the city. He learnt that she was more interested in anthropology than paintings, in the various parks and gardens than gilded palaces. Her shoulders were still tense, her smiles smaller as they chatted their way through tiramisu, as he paid the bill and helped her into her coat. They stepped out into the brisk night air, the light breeze's bite a shock after the restaurant's warmth.

"Can I walk you back to your place?" He asked, and she hesitated slightly, her breath misting in the air. "You can escort me back to the shop if you like," she offered, conveniently omitting the fact that she lived above the store. However sheltered she might have been growning up, she clearly knew better than to give a virtual stranger her address. Not that he didn't already have it.

He fell into step beside her as they moved down Broadway, the shop lights guiding them. He could see the sign for Lit Happens, the bookshop where she worked, glowing up the road, a prime corner location sandwiched between a fish and chip shop and a clothing store. Despite the chill, it was a lovely night, crisp and clear, a faint scattering of stars visible above the illuminated shop signs and rows of Edwardian buildings that towered above them, a nod to the area's history.

The crash came without warning. A squeal of brakes that raised the hairs on the back of his neck and had him dragging Ana away from the road, under the awning of the supermarket they were passing, followed by a god-awful screech and tear of metal as the car wrapped itself around one of the old fashioned streetlights mere metres from them. The smell hit him first, acrid black smoke pouring from the engine as the front of the car burst into flames. Shouts flooded the air and he turned to see people running towards the vehicle, the wrench of metal as the twisted door was pulled open and the driver hauled out, coughing and spluttering into the street, dragged away from the burning wreck.

Icy cold flooded Theo's body, the smell and the sounds holding him in place, familiar and brutal. Fire. Pain. Danger. He forced his eyes shut, but the memories rushed him, flashing into reality behind his closed lids. The dry heat of the desert, the scent of burning fabric and flesh, the screams of innocents. He couldn't breathe. His lungs tightened, burning for release, air trapped behind the lump in his throat. Not now. Not this. Not this sick, twisted feeling taking over, leaking itself out through his pores in hot stripes that ran down his forehead and off his nose. The pavement was hard and cold under his hands and knees, miles from the warm give of Afghan sand, and he pressed down, trying to fight through the memories to the grit of a London street under his palms. He didn't remember dropping. Theo opened his mouth, desperate for oxygen. Nothing happened. He wrestled through the pain, through the fear that coated his tongue in thick ropes, through the sharp edges of the flashback that sliced at him, his brain ripping its way through the patchwork of the past in a messy, bloody battle to send the message to his throat.

Work. Work for me.

The lump shifted, just a little, just to the side. Just enough that the air trapped inside him could come rushing out, leaving his body in a violent exhalation. He dragged another breath in, desperate and fast. And another. Until the oxygen took over, cleared the worst of the images from his mind, pushing them far enough into the dark corners that he could come back to himself, shaking and panting down on the frozen footpath.

"Theo?"

He grunted.

"Theo, there's some water here. Take a sip when you can." A plastic bottle was placed next to him, glowing in the downward fluorescence of the supermarket light. Ana's hand was on his back. No stroking, not petting him like a skittish horse. Just... there. Solid. He focused on that, on the slight pressure against his lower spine, the press of his shirt and coat to his sweaty skin in that one spot, and he worked outwards from there.

Ribs? Fine. Legs? Fine. Arms? Fine. Head? Well, that's another story isn't it?

He didn't look up, fumbling for the water bottle that sat already opened by his hand. He tried to lift it to his lips, but missed. A thin stream of water splashed down over his other arm, the one supporting him, and trickled off his hand onto the rough asphalt.

"Here." She was touching him again, turning him, arranging his weak limbs like a doll until he sat cross legged on the path, one of her arms around him. "Okay? Let's try again." She lifted the bottle to his lips this time and he drank, the cool relief flooding his dry mouth. He swallowed it down gratefully, reaching up to take it from her.

By the time he'd finished drinking, the ambulance had arrived. The driver of the car was being examined, the supermarket workers had finished handing out water to the crowd of onlookers and the crowd was beginning to disperse.

Shame crawled in, slithering over the dark patches where fear had been, filling up the hollows in his body.

Nightmares were one thing - in his bed, in the dark, alone. But this? This epic loss of control in a public street? The kind that brought him to his knees, sweating and shaking and far removed from the man he'd worked extremely hard to turn himself into. Humiliation rose in hot waves. The ambulance officers were shooting him curious glances, as well they might. He hadn't been hurt. Ana hadn't been hurt. Neither of them had been pulled from a burning car. Yet there they were, huddled together on the cold asphalt, victims to his treacherous mind.

The thought burned. Theo Miller was no victim. Not to his druggie mother and her neglectful parenting. Not to the foster care system. Definitely not to post-traumatic stress disorder, the name the army shrinks had given to the demons that had taken up residence in his mind after a decade of sending bombs and drones and information into battles across airwaves and watching the results spark riots and revolutions across the world in service to his country.

He would beat this. He was a survivor.

The thought pulled him to his feet, spine straight, and he reached down absentmindedly to help Ana up. The first touch of her hand against his pulled him back. He looked down, marvelling at the way her hand fit in his. Softer and darker, the press of their skin together sending warmth racing down his arm that had nothing to do with the crash or his unacceptable reaction to it. Their chests brushed together as he helped her to her feet and for the first time since the squeal of tyres had echoed down Broadway he looked at her. Her eyes were huge, her face drawn and paler than it had looked at dinner. Her top lip was pinker than the bottom, which sported no sign of lipstick, no doubt due to the way her teeth worried at her lower lip as she gazed up at him.

"Are you okay?"

He started to say he was, but she stepped closer, their hands still linked. Her other hand moved up to cup his cheek. She was only an inch or two shorter than him in her boots and the front of their bodies pressed together as she studied him. This close he could see flecks of gold within her dark irises and he knew she must be seeing him just as clearly, his vulnerability no doubt written like a script across his face.

"Not really." His voice was hoarse. "But I will be." If he said it enough, it might even be true.

Ana's face softened at his honesty and she nodded once, dropping her hand from his face and stepping back. The cool air moved into the space between them and he missed her immediately.

"Good," she murmured.

"Come on," he replied, stuffing one hand into his jacket pocket, the other one still clutching hers. "Let's get you home."

THREE

The shop bell jangled as the customer left, and Ana spritzed the counter with disinfectant, wiping it down in quick, efficient circles.

"Bit tense?" Gert inquired.

Ana shot the older woman her best fake smile.

"Don't try that shite on me, love. How'd your date with the pretty boy go last night?"

Ana thought about it. As if she'd been doing anything else since Theo farewelled her on the threshold of the shop door last night and strode off into the night, his jaw as tight as his butt. "It was interesting."

"Interesting? Did he cover you in melted cheese and play fondue with his chorizo?"

Ana stared at her in disbelief. "What does that even mean?"

Gert cackled. "Oh, my sweet innocent."

Ana shook her head, dispelling any unwelcome thoughts of dairy goods where they didn't belong. "No, it was okay. Dinner was nice. Lots of questions though."

"The man you asked on a date had the audacity to try to get to know you? Bastard."

Ana shrugged, her inexperience prickling at her. "Is that normal? I haven't really dated much."

"It's normal," Gert assured her, much to Ana's relief. She might be sixty years younger than her boss, but she was positive Gert's knowledge of modern dating practices was superior to her own. "If he only wanted to tip your wicket he wouldn't have bothered with dinner. Just swiped you on one of those dating apps and sent you a picture of his johnson looking like an angry mole rat," the older woman added.

Ana pulled her phone out of her jeans pocket and googled mole rats.

"Holy cow," she said, recoiling from her screen in horror.

"Mmm," Gert nodded sagely.

"And then when he was walking me home, there was a car accident."

"Ooh, Janice told me about that. Good thing they got it all cleaned up by the time the shops opened this morning."

"It almost hit us. It was a bit scary."

"You alright, then?"

"Yeah. Not a great way to end a date, though."

Gert smirked at her. "Maybe next time."

"There might not be a next time. I might have been a bit short with him. Plus, we almost got mown down by a car. I didn't think guys liked drama."

Gert shrugged. "Depends who's on the stage. My last husband would have walked over hot coals if he thought it'd get me out of a grump."

"How many husbands have you had?"

"Three. The first was a mistake, the second was an

escape from the first one, and the third was the last one I'll ever have."

"Because he was the best?"

"Because I'm too old to be wasting my time on men," Gert snapped. "Also because he was the best," she added in a softer tone, and Ana watched as a dreamy smile flitted across her face for the barest hint of a second. Yup, Gert's third husband must have been something.

She was still mulling over her date with Theo, on her knees, tidying the religious memoir section, when the bell rang again.

"Ana?" Gert called from the front of the store. "Delivery for you."

Giving the section a half-hearted shove to straighten the books up - not that it mattered, it wasn't an oft-visited section - she stood and headed towards the counter.

Except the counter was obscured by the biggest bunch of flowers she'd ever seen outside of church.

"Those can't be for me."

"That's what the card says." Gert waved a slip of card-board in the air, before bringing it closer to her face and squinting at it. "*To Ana. Last night didn't quite go to plan. I'd love to try again. T.* He's put his phone number here too."

"I didn't think it went that well," Ana said, dazed, as she moved closer to examine the blooms.

"Went well enough for him to send you tulips the day before New Year's Eve. Those'd be imported, then?" Gert directed her question to the left and Ana noticed the wizened old delivery man still standing there, staring at Gert like she'd hung the moon.

He nodded enthusiastically. "From The Netherlands."

"I've never seen tulips in real life before," Ana admitted,

and the old man - Jorge, he introduced himself as - rushed to explain the significance of the flower.

"Tulips symbolise deep love and also rebirth or new beginnings. White flowers themselves mean forgiveness, as well as respect and honour. Your young man," Jorge coughed softly, "he asked for something that would apologise to you and ask for a second chance. I gave him some options and he chose this one."

Ana studied the flowers again, turning the words over in her head. Deep love was out of the question, of course, but the idea of new beginnings appealed to her. Without knowing it, Theo had sent her flowers that represented her own journey, while respectfully asking for another shot. Flowers that he'd chosen himself, with Jorge's help.

"Interesting," she murmured.

Jorge hesitated before speaking.

"I think you should give him another chance. He seemed sincere."

"Oi!" Gert swatted at him with a rolled up magazine. "You don't get a say in this."

"Yes, ma'am." He stepped back immediately, eyes downcast.

"Whether or not the woman wants to call him is up to her."

"Of course."

"Even when it's completely obvious that he's not just some dickhead trying to get into her pants, and he's dropped near a hundred quid on fancy flowers after one crappy date, we've still got to let her make her own decision. She can't be swayed by the likes of us."

"You're right, Ms Clifford."

"So," Gert turned back to Ana, mischief gleaming in her eyes. "What are you going to do?"

Ana shot them both a firm look. Gert grinned. Jorge didn't notice, he was busy glancing sideways at Gert out of the corner of his eye.

"I think I'll take my break now. In my flat." She plucked the card out of Gert's hand on her way past.

"Fifteen minutes," Gert hollered at her back as she headed up the stairs to the right of the counter. "I'm not paying you to be seduced."

Ana smirked as she unlocked her flat door and let herself in. Pulling her phone out once more, she flopped onto her pale blue bedspread and unlocked the screen.

"Crap."

The summons had arrived. At least, that's what she assumed it was - an email with an Avalian tagline, sent from Iosefa, the assistant to her biological father, King Tama. Guilt, anger and hurt swirled in her stomach, a noxious combination. It would be easy to ignore it, to trash the email and pretend she'd never laid eyes on it. Her thumb twitched with the temptation. But no, this version of herself was braver than that. She opened it.

Miss Oliana,

It has come to my attention that you are in the United Kingdom. As you know, all international travel plans for members of the royal family need prior approval from His Majesty.

Ana snorted at the blatant lie. Her brothers travelled internationally on a whim, often using Tama's private plane.

Your presence in Avali is required at once. Please call me to disclose your exact location and I will begin preparations for your travel.

Regards,

Iosefa Lupi

Executive Assistant to His Royal Majesty, King Tama of Avali.

NOT A CHANCE, Iosefa. They had no idea where in the UK she was. Otherwise Ana was in no doubt that there would already be a boarding pass with her name on it. The request to call was clearly an additional attempt to track her location. It wouldn't take long. Just accessing the email had probably left her position flagged openly in the world of cybersecurity or whatever it was. But she'd be damned if she let her father's loyal basset hound call her home like an unruly pup. She'd been a puppet too many times in the games the royal family had been playing for the past two and a half decades and she was tired of having her strings pulled. When they found her, there'd be nothing but threads for them to cling to. She was going to do this, be the best, liveliest Ana she could *while* she could. Deleting the email, she navigated to her contacts, and beneath the two names already there, Gert and her brother Sio, she entered Theo's number, mouthing the numbers to herself as she typed it in and pulled up the messaging icon.

Hi Theo. I'd like to try again too. Tomorrow night?

INTERFERING OLD BASTARD.

Theo fumed at the message he'd received from King Tama's minion.

GOOD MORNING MR MILLER.

. . .

WE ARE *aware of your arrangement with His Highness Prince Aleki regarding protection of his sister, Her Royal Highness Princess Oliana. This situation is now being dealt with by the family. Please consider your contract voided. The agreed upon amount has been transferred to your bank account.*

Have a pleasant day.

Regards,

Iosefa Lupi

Executive Assistant to His Royal Majesty, King Tama of Avali.

ANA WOULD BE off like a shot if Avalian personnel turned up, no matter who employed them. Theo's own employment matter was clear - Aleki had hired him and signed the contract, therefore Aleki was the only one who could fire him. Until that happened, he was going to do his job to the best of his ability. Provided Ana ever spoke to him again.

He dropped his head to his desktop, narrowly missing his keyboard. He'd fucked it right up last night. It was the first time in months a flashback had happened while he was awake, the first time since he left the army. They mostly came at night, and those were rarely seen by others. On the odd occasion when he'd been sharing a bed with someone it was easy to write it off as a simple nightmare, and he'd upped his chances by not sleeping with anyone more than once since his fun dalliance with Clare's friend Jeremy had finished. Mostly because Jeremy had seen one too many 'nightmares' and asked if he needed to speak to someone. Now they mostly communicated by tagging each other in photos of baby animals and sending each other pictures of increasingly inappropriate attire for Clare's wedding.

His phone dinged and his heart leapt at the message from Ana. It was normal to be excited about a life-changing professional opportunity, he reminded himself. Nothing to do with her gorgeous smile, her dark eyes, the lush curves of her body. Nothing at all.

It's New Year's Eve tomorrow night, he messaged back. *Do you have plans?*

No plans, she responded. *But there is something I'd like to do.*

What's that?

I want to stay out all night. I want an adventure that lasts until morning.

Theo's brow cocked. It wasn't a wild request from a twenty-four year old, but there was certainly an element of strength to it - she was making it clear that she didn't want to come back to his place.

Any particular adventure you're keen to undertake?

Surprise me.

A chuckle bubbled out of his chest. He liked this version of her, forthright and feisty, miles from the picture of the demure young lady Aleki and Manu had painted in their description of their sister.

I'll pick you up at seven, he replied, and went about organising surprises.

THEO ALMOST SWALLOWED his tongue when Ana opened the bookshop door right on seven the next night. She was wearing a chunky cream sweater dress studded with pearls that hit just above her knee, her black coat folded over her elbow. Miles of long brown calves led to black ankle boots. Her lips and nails were bright red and she'd done something that made her eyes look even bigger. She grinned at him, excitement shining in her eyes, and Theo felt a jolt in his chest. God she was beautiful, full of life and joy and happy to see him of all people. He'd be the luckiest bastard alive if it wasn't for the nagging pressure at the top of his spine reminding him that spending time with her was a job, a job he desperately needed to secure high profile clients for the business.

"You look incredible," he said, because it was true, and her smile widened. She was like the sun, pulling him in, drawing him towards her until he was close enough to brush his lips against her soft cheek.

"So do you," she offered and he smiled, glad that he'd worn the one tuxedo Liam had talked him into as a business expense in their early days of operation. Speaking of business expenses... "Shall we?" Theo motioned to the street, where their driver stood next to a shiny black sedan.

He followed her into the car and they buckled in as the driver pulled smoothly away from the kerb.

"Where are we going?" Ana bounced in her seat, child-like in her excitement.

"It's a surprise, remember? Don't worry though, the first stop isn't far." They pulled to a stop less than three minutes later. "Come on, then," Theo laughed at Ana's wide-eyed gaze and helped her out of the car.

"We've just driven around the corner."

"Pretty much," he agreed. "This is Alexandra Palace."

She gazed up at the impressive stone facade, the huge circular stained glass window. Behind her the lights of London glowed, rows and rows of stars thrown onto an inky blanket, and the BT tower, rising like an obnoxious phallic antenna. "Palaces aren't really my thing, remember?"

"This one is different," Theo assured her, placing a hand on her back and steering her up the wide steps. Once inside, they turned at the first left and Ana squealed in delight.

"Ice skating!"

"Have you ever been?"

"No, never!"

The rink took up a huge hall, surrounded on two sides by tall arches of bevelled glass that let skaters look out on the grounds and the city below. The same windows were at the back of the room, separating the rink from an internal corridor, and behind the entrance they'd walked in were rows of spectator seating. Theo handed over twenty quid for admission and skate hire and followed Ana to the low seats next to the rink to change their footwear. The space was still decorated for Christmas, lit up in a rainbow of colours, fairy lights strung across the high ceilings. The rink itself was quiet, a few couples and individuals scattered around the ice.

"Are you going to be alright in that dress?" he asked, as Ana stood to her feet and leaned left and right on the thin blades, testing her balance.

"Absolutely," she replied confidently. "Come on!" She clunked noisily to the ice entrance and he followed, somewhat graceless himself. Together they clutched at the barrier, small steps, testing glides.

"Have you done this before?" Ana asked, shooting him a suspicious glance out of the corner of her eye when he went for a hands-free glide forward. "Are you one of those men who thinks it's fun to bring a woman to an activity she's unfamiliar with to show off your superior skills?"

"Not at all," Theo promised. "There may have been a short rollerblading stint in my teens, but I can promise you that has no bearing on my skating skills now." As if on cue, he wobbled, one arm shooting out to catch the barrier, using his upper body strength to hold his torso upright as his lower body lurched back and forth like a marionette mid-seizure.

They got the hang of it eventually, skating slow circles around the rink. He reached out to steady her at one point, catching her hand as she faltered, keeping his larger one wrapped around hers. Ana's smile grew in direct proportion to her confidence, bigger and brighter with each lap of the ice as she attempted tighter turns and increased speed. They skated for an hour or so before returning their skates to the rental kiosk and putting their own shoes on. When they stepped outside, coats buttoned tight, the driver was waiting for them with a blanket and a steaming thermos of hot chocolate and they sat on the wide steps of the palace and drank it looking over London.

"Why are we staying out all night?" Theo asked, as the wind picked up strands of her hair and they danced towards him. The subtle scent of coconut, and something heavier, richer, wound itself around him and he scooched closer, leaving only an inch between their thighs.

"It's on my list," Ana answered, shifting slightly. Her leg touched his, sending a frisson up his thigh, directly to his groin. She didn't move, just let it rest there, the press of her flesh against his jeans under the blanket scorching him through the thick fabric.

"What list?" Theo rasped.

"I have a list." There was a determined set to her jaw as she gazed out over the sparkling landscape below. "Kind of a bucket list, but instead of achieving it all before I die, I'm doing it on this trip."

There we go. She did have a plan.

"So what's on this list?" Theo kept his voice light.

She shot him a glance under shimmering eyelids, and he took a sip of his hot chocolate, schooling his face into mild curiosity.

"I want to stay out all night," she relented. "That's the first thing. Well, technically, cutting my hair was the first thing so I suppose it's the second. I want to attend a protest. Go skinny dipping. Get a tattoo."

Theo nodded. "Do they have to be done in order?"

She shook her head and that rich scent wrapped itself around him again. He drew in a deep breath, relishing the combination of it with the crisp night air.

"Five items," he said.

"Yup." Her voice was firm. "Just the five."

"That's doable." None of them were dangerous. None of them would put her at risk - depending on the protest of course. He could safely report back to Aleki that his little sister wanted nothing more than a holiday to let loose in a way that had clearly been stymied by her traditional upbringing.

Except... what happened next? He walked away and left her to it? They might be low-risk activities, but she'd still be doing them by herself, in one of the largest cities in the world. His chest pinched. "Do you need a hand with any of them?" He forced a casual tone and was rewarded with an assessing look.

"I don't know," Ana mused, her eyes dancing with repressed laughter. "You've got that buttoned up thing going on and you're definitely older than me. You might not be able to keep up."

"I'm thirty," Theo protested.

"Ancient," she grinned. "Practically prehistoric."

"How old are you then?" he demanded, as if he didn't

already know. As if he couldn't rattle off her birthdate, star sign and the results of her last physical at the drop of a hat.

"Twenty-four," she replied.

"A mere babe in the woods," he snorted. "Do not cite the dark party magic at me, child. I was there when it was written. You know nothing about true revelry."

"That's true," Ana agreed easily. "Maybe I could use a guide. Someone as seasoned as you. Let's consider tonight your audition. If you impress me, I might invite you along on the rest of my adventures."

"A challenge!" Theo lifted his fist in the air. "Let us onward then!" He began gathering up the blanket. "Come, my lady. Your night of adventure awaits." Standing, he held out an arm, elbow crooked, while she looked up at him as though he was mad. Hell, he might as well be. She'd already seen him at his weakest, shaking on the street. He should run as fast as he could from her, from the echo of humiliation at being brought to his knees in front of her, his vulnerability laid open like a specimen for her to poke at. But all he wanted was to help her - to take the small, simple dreams this clever, witty, warm woman held, and make them her reality. Gladness burst inside him. He'd made arrangements for their night, of course. Plans and an itinerary. Called in a favour from Liam, even. But knowing now that this was part of her wider dream, that this night would be one that she'd carry with her as she aged, one of the memories of her time in London that she'd look back on and cherish, he was pleased he'd put the effort in. As she stood and linked her arm through his, he looked deep into her brown eyes.

"If it's an adventure you want, Ana, it's an adventure you'll get."

FOUR

They went dancing next. In a packed club down in South London, Latin music licking at them, a sticky beat that thrummed and pulsed as the crowd swayed and swirled in a rainbow cacophony. Ana could dance, of course. There wasn't an Avalian girl alive with full use of their limbs who hadn't been raised with dance as an essential language, along with English and their native tongue. But Theo surprised her. The fluidity of his hips, the easy way he spun her out and pulled her back against his chest. They danced for what seemed like hours, beginner steps compared to the couples that whirled around them, but quick and natural with limited foot-stomping and clumsiness. Eventually Ana folded, the swarmed floor and intricate footwork combining with the weight of her dress to exhaust her. It was only a wool-acrylic blend she'd had to get an advance on her pay to purchase especially in a high street shop, but the high neck and long sleeves were no match for a sweaty, writhing dancefloor and a partner like Theo with his Energizer Bunny stamina.

They stumbled out onto the street, hands linked, the cool air a relief on her moist brow.

"What's the time?" she asked as they fell into the waiting car. *Chauffeured vehicles are definitely the way to go.* Briefly, she remembered that Aleki had a private car and driver, but she pushed the thought away. The potential perks of royal life in Avali weren't enough to lure her back before her time here was up.

Theo checked his watch, one of those huge ones with a thousand time zones and sea levels and GPS that all modern men with MacGyver fantasies owned. "Almost eleven. Westminster, please," he instructed the driver.

"An hour left," Ana mused. She rolled her head to the side, eyeing him across the wide leather seat. "Got your New Year's resolution ready?"

Heat turned his hazel eyes darker as he ran his gaze up and down the length of her body. When they met hers again, they were a potent mix of toffee and emerald. Lust hit her low in her abdomen, buzzing out along her limbs, and she squeezed her thighs together. They'd been pressed together in the club, his chest to her back, the solid weight of his arms around her body, but somehow it was in the dim light of the car's interior, not even touching, that gave life to the intimacy between them. It swelled, reaching out like a living thing, tendrils curling around her, heightening her awareness, pulling her until she leaned in towards Theo. Theo and his hot, perfect gaze. Theo and his strong, solid body. Ana's nipples stiffened under the promise in his eyes. She shifted slightly, moving a fraction of an inch towards him and a slow grin spread across his face. He reached out and ran one finger down the curve of her cheek, a whisper light touch.

"Don't worry about me, sweetheart." His voice was like

warm cream, thick and luscious, spilling over her. "I'm ready for midnight."

A shiver ran up her body. She clasped her hands together in her lap, staring down at the nails. She'd painted them red this afternoon in her little flat with the heater on full bore, wrapped in her duvet while Christmas movies played in the background. They slid through the darkened streets full of revellers towards Westminster. The area was lit up in gold when they arrived, lights shining up at the towering buildings she'd only ever seen on TV or websites. Partygoers lined the streets, the sensible ones bundled up against the cold. Theo helped her out of the car and led her down to a pier, the London Eye winking at them as it moved in a slow revolution across the river. At the bottom of the pier, he held her hand and helped her into a small vessel. It wasn't one of the usual river tour boats - those were already lit up along the river, stuffed with silhouettes. It was smaller, a little glassed-in area at the front to protect them from the wind. Theo unlocked it and drew her in. Inside the tiny cabin was a pile of blankets, a picnic basket, a bottle of champagne resting in an ice bucket and a pair of tall glasses.

"How very organised," Ana murmured, and he shrugged.

"I like things organised."

No shit. It was glaringly obvious. The tap of his foot as they'd waited for the car outside Alexandra Palace, the schedule of the evening's events. Even his appearance hinted at a man who liked things according to plan - short hair, almost military in style, a clean-shaven jaw. Precise. Fuss-free. No time for distractions.

Then why is he here with you? Ana wasn't stupid. Despite the fact that her parents had encouraged her to stay at home and focus on charity work rather than attend university, she'd been one of the top students in her class. Anyone with half a brain would look at her right now and see her as a distraction. That was the point of this, the whole idea of shucking her heritage and breaking free was born from the need to escape the endless tedium of her life in Avali. Mind you, maybe that was it. Maybe Theo's life was so controlled, so fine-tuned, that a girl like her - like the London version of her at least - was the perfect antidote. Maybe he needed to blow off a little steam too. Maybe he'd be interested in blowing it off in the bedroom.

Ridiculous.

She chided herself for the thought even as it passed through her mind. She couldn't bring up sex as it pertained to her list when she'd shared it with him. When it was right there, number six, written in perfect black ink on a pristine white page. A tangible goal. One that she hadn't mentioned, lest the giant gorgeous hunk currently pouring her a glass of champagne thought she was silly. What made her think she'd be able to proposition him? People who couldn't talk about sex, probably shouldn't be having it, but gods she wanted to. The more time she spent with Theo and his careful, caring, coordinated plans, the more she wanted to do it with him specifically.

"Here you go." Ana started at Theo's voice, accepting the champagne flute from him.

"Thank you." She took a sip. It was delicious, crisp and fresh, the bubbles dancing on her tongue, with a surprisingly acidic finish. Her parents were teetotallers and sermons on the dangers of alcohol were part of the soundtrack of her life. As far as Ana was concerned, the golden liquid shimmering in her glass tasted like freedom.

She moved to the right of the boat, keeping out of the

way as he untied it from the pier before taking up position at the steering wheel on the left, deftly manoeuvring the small craft through the water until they had a direct view of Tower Bridge arching across the water. Theo spun the boat until they were facing away and pushed a few buttons before grabbing the blankets and picnic basket.

"Come on."

She followed him out onto the open-air deck and by the gods, it was freezing.

"Uh, Theo?" Ana ventured. "I'm not sure if you noticed, but this outfit was kind of designed for elegance, not the elements."

"Oh, I noticed." Theo waggled his brows at her and she bit back a laugh. "Don't worry, there's a plan for that." He patted the seat next to him, where he'd spread out a blanket. She settled onto it and he covered her legs with another, wrapping a third around both their shoulders until they were cocooned together, only the crisp breeze on her face and hands as she lifted the champagne glass to her lips hinting at the frigid London temperature.

Theo unpacked the picnic basket, revealing a pre-prepared cheese board and a small side plate of cured meats he'd clearly fixed for her, given his own vegetarianism. Her heart swelled, feeling a size too big for her chest as he settled the dish down on the blankets between them.

They grazed in silence as they watched the crowds swell along the banks of the river, under the golden glow of the Houses of Parliament and Big Ben on one side, and the Embankment on the other. The wind fluttered around them and tossed strands of Ana's hair across her face and she tucked them back behind her ears, still marvelling at the shorter length. Her mother was going to be horrified - Ana had never been allowed to cut her hair shorter than to the small of her back. Her virginity was going to be the same, she decided, biting into a cracker smothered in brie and quince paste. Not as obvious as the hair, nobody would be able to tell, but she would know. Know that when she returned to Avali she would be different, in a way that couldn't be reversed, through a means that she'd chosen and had total control over. She slid a sly glance at Theo again, and he caught her eye, smiling at her with all those straight white teeth.

Gods, he's pretty.

Different from the island men. Not any more handsome, or any better mannered. But different. And she knew with sudden certainty that if she had her way, he would be hers. He was her choice.

"The fireworks are about to start," he said, checking his watch.

"I've never seen fireworks in real life," she confessed. Avali had strict rules around the import of fireworks due to the fire risk and the danger to animals. Theo eyed her in surprise. "Well, get up there. Have a look." He helped her wiggle out of their blanket burrow, placing their food and the now-empty glasses on the deck. She moved quickly to the rail that ran along the deck, gripping the cool metal as she gazed towards the bridge that rose into the dark. The air changed as Theo stood behind her, close but not touching. A sizzle of electricity might as well have arced between their bodies, she was so in tune with him.

"Are you excited?" His breath warmed her ear and she fought off a shiver that had nothing to do with the weather.

"Yes." She turned and he was right there, looming into her view as the countdown started in the background.

Ten... nine... eight...

The rail pressed into the small of her back, a cool band

through the wool fabric of her dress. Theo placed his hands on the same rail, one on each side of her body, hemming her in as the small boat swayed in the wake of larger vessels trawling down the river.

Seven... six... five...

Their breaths misted, mingling in the chill of the air.

Four... three... two...

Theo reached out and caught an errant strand of her hair between his fingers, sliding his hand down to cup her chin.

One.

He brushed his lips across hers, soft and gentle. Once more, a featherlight touch that dizzied her. A little moan escaped her when he pulled back again. She looked up into his eyes, the lights of the fireworks bringing out the gold and green in his pupils, until they were all she could see, soft and glowing and looking at her like she was the most perfect thing in the world. He moved to step back but she fisted the thick wool of his jumper and tugged. He stumbled forward a half-step until the length of his body was pressed against hers.

"Again?" His quiet question hung in the air but it was louder to her than the noisy revelry of the celebrations taking place around them.

"Again," she said. She angled her head to meet him this time. His lips were firmer on hers now, a gorgeous press that lit her up from the inside, and the butterflies in her stomach turned to fire, molten liquid that spread, heating her limbs as she wound her arms around his neck and pressed herself harder against him. His tongue traced the seam of her lips and she opened her mouth eagerly, giving him licence to lick into her, for their tongues to tangle in a sensual dance as Theo banded an arm around her lower back. His lips left hers and she whimpered a protest before they found purchase again on her neck, travelling in a warm line between a spot behind her ear and the place where her dress met her skin. She shuddered, holding him tight and let her head roll back to allow him further exploration. His tongue flicked out, lapping at the soft skin of her collarbone and all the heat and passion in her body shot south. Ana shuddered, her thighs rubbing together as if she could fill the aching space between them alone. Theo reversed his trail of fire and she angled her head to catch his mouth again, her own tongue dancing out to meet his, revelling in the taste of him, champagne and something else, something darker and more primal. Adrenaline surged through her bloodstream, the combination of the kiss and her own agency leaving her giddy.

Theo pulled back slowly, lighting one, two, three lingering kisses on her eager mouth, soft, soulful kisses that added to her headiness. They untangled themselves and she clutched at the railing beside her to steady herself as she took him in, his hazel eyes a little wild in the reflection of the rainbow fireworks that still sparkled overhead.

He swallowed hard, his throat working as they continued to stare at each other and somewhere in the haze of desire that blurred their surroundings she felt a spike of triumph.

I made him feel like that.

"Happy New Year," she managed, her voice sounding like a shout in the quiet space between them.

"Yeah," he muttered, golden eyes boring into hers. "Happy New Year, Ana."

THEO FLOPPED BACK on his bed, chest heaving, his breath sawing in and out in hulking gasps. Another sleep, another nightmare. Sweat covered his body, despite the fact that his sheets tangled around his feet. Slowly he concentrated on getting his breathing under control. It wasn't even night, for Christ's sake. Early morning light peeked around the corners of his curtain. After they returned Liam's mate's boat to the pier, they'd wandered the streets a little, her hand wrapped in his as they strolled under the fairy lights of Covent Garden through to Leicester Square, where they'd bought burgers and fries at a chain restaurant and eaten them off sticky plastic tables while sitting on hard chairs. In the pale dawn, he'd walked her back to the bookshop from the East Finchley tube station, rose gold-tipped clouds drifting in the soft lavender sky above them, gilding her features as she swung their linked hands together. All throughout it, the memory of their kiss had played in his mind on a loop. The soft yield of her lips, the way she'd pulled him to her. He'd been half-hard since midnight.

This is not good.

She was about to be his best friend's sister-in-law. He and Clare had celebrated every major life achievement together since their teens. There was no way he'd be able to avoid Ana once she returned to Avali. Clare and Manu's wedding was in September, for one thing. Surely they'd both be present there.

Anxiety roiled in his chest. Things had gone too far last night. A peck on the lips was fine, he'd reasoned with himself as he stood looking at her in the boat. Expected, even. It was midnight on New Year's Eve. But she'd gone and pulled his jumper and he'd fallen into her. Fallen further than he should have, if the butterflies in his stomach and the way he'd snuck glances at her as they'd wandered the early morning streets of London, Ana wrapped in his coat and him brushing her dark hair out of her eyes was any indication.

This was not a part of the plan.

Rolling over, he yanked the sheets up as he grabbed his phone off his bedside table, thumbing in the number of his emotional touchstone.

"Hello?"

"Happy New Year, Clare Bear." The band in Theo's chest loosened a little at the sound of her voice. He'd tried pulling back a little when Manu came on the scene, until she'd rung up and yelled at him that they were a damn family, and they still needed regular catch-ups regardless of their relationship status. To be honest, he'd been proud of her for calling him on it, because Clare wasn't one for confrontation, despite her no-nonsense attitude. In their foster family, she'd always been curled up in her room with a book trying to avoid any conflict, while he'd been yelling and putting his fist through drywall the first year he was there, before he'd learnt to shut down his emotions. To take the pain and helplessness he felt and lock it down tight under layers of routine and control and discipline. His coding had given him an escape and the army had given him focus, but the combination of the two and the way he'd been used had taken something from him too. Something he was still working to get back.

"Happy New Year, Bond. How is spy life?" His best friend laughed down the phone at him. "Have you bought a dinner jacket and an Aston Martin yet?"

Theo grinned, relaxing further into their easy banter. "It's being detailed. Can you believe the dealership tried to sell it to me with beige leather interior?"

"Animals."

"Did you and Manu do anything exciting to ring in the New Year?"

"Not really." He could practically hear her shrug. "We spent the night at Aleki and Stella's. Homemade pizzas and newborn snuggles."

"How is the baby?"

"So sweet," Clare sighed happily. "Makes me consider having one."

Theo stilled. "That's new." Clare had always claimed kids were not in her future. His brain worked, trying to slot this new piece of information into his Clare file.

"I'm thinking about it, but I haven't decided yet," she offered quietly. "A lot of the things I thought when I was younger were based on the idea that I'd always be alone. Now that I'm not, I'm reconsidering a few ideas."

"That makes sense." His voice betrayed none of his concern - Clare's walls would shoot up at the speed of light if she thought he was worried about her - but the idea that falling in love could alter previously unshakeable facets of his best friend's life didn't make sense to him. He heard a masculine rumble on the other end of the phone before Clare spoke again. "Manu's going to get Aleki and you can fill them in on the Oliana situation."

Theo hadn't called for that reason, but it seemed like he didn't have a say now. Rolling out of bed, he reached for his clothes where they lay folded on the chair next to his bed. An old army habit that proved its convenience right now. It was one thing to chat to Clare while sprawled in bed wearing nothing but sweatpants, but he'd be damned if he delivered a formal report to a client without being properly dressed. He yanked jeans and a sweater on while Clare talked about the new position she was starting as scientific director at her fertility clinic after the holidays. By the time

Manu's voice sounded in the background again, he was seated at his computer desk, screens on, hair combed.

He was glad he had when Aleki appeared on his monitor. The prince was wearing a business shirt and looked fresh and alert. Manu hovered behind him, hair sleep-mussed, clad only in a sleeveless training top, but that was par for the course for Clare's fiancé when he was relaxing at home. The first hint of a night out though, and he was dressed to the nines.

"Miller." Aleki's accent was sharp. "What have you got for us?"

Theo cleared his throat and pushed his discomfort aside. This was what he was paid for. And the Esera brothers were paying a lot.

"Your sister is living in a neighbourhood in North London. She has secured a safe place to live and employment in the same building."

"Why?"

"As far as I can ascertain, she has some personal goals she would like to achieve before she returns to Avali. None of these are of any particular concern in terms of her personal safety or the reputation of the Avalian royal family."

"She's safe?"

"Yes. Her building is secure and actively alarmed. She is the only resident and only her employer, an elderly woman, has building access. She has never arrived before eight in the morning or stayed past six since surveillance began. Your sister predominantly spends evenings in her room or exploring the local area. All communications indicate she is here alone, for the express purpose of a holiday." His skin crawled as he spoke, a thin layer of invisible filth settling over him as he discussed Ana with her brothers. He kept it as vague as he could while still fulfilling his professional responsibility. No need to mention she was exploring the local areas with him more often than not. The last thing he needed was one of them suspecting his loyalty was split. The company could never recover from that type of rumour if it got out.

"Good." Aleki nodded decisively. "You will continue to tail her and ensure she is not doing anything that would cause problems. Written reports will be delivered weekly."

Theo's stomach twisted and he took a deep breath through his nose to settle himself.

"What about socialising?" Manu asked in the video's background. "How can we trust the people she's spending time with?"

Theo sucked in some air and promptly choked on it.

"Are you okay?" Clare popped up in the corner of his screen.

"Yup, yup." Eyes running, he took a swig of the water bottle he'd filled and set alongside his desk yesterday afternoon before he picked up Ana. Just in case the champagne had hit him a little too hard. No such worries there, not when he'd been kiss-drunk since midnight.

"Ah, I don't think that's necessary," he offered, and both Esera brothers frowned at him in dark-browed unison. "The only person I've seen her speak to outside of her customers is her employer, who must be nearing her mid-eighties."

"Nevertheless, if you could run a background search on the woman, we'd be grateful. Add it to our bill," Aleki instructed.

"Sure." Theo's voice was faint. "Anything else?" *Please, please, wrap this up before you notice I've got the hots for your sister.*

"Not from me," Aleki said, and Theo sent up a silent

prayer to a god he didn't believe in. "I'll leave you to chat to Clare." The prince rose and Theo watched the crotch of his finely tailored pants move across the front of the screen before Clare plopped back into the seat he'd occupied. Manu dropped a kiss on top of her head and there was a pause while she waited for the door to click shut behind the brothers.

"I'm glad you've seen her," Clare confided. "These guys have been losing their minds with worry. Can't blame her for doing a runner while she still can, though."

Theo's hackles raised, almost out of habit more than anything else. "Is future princess life not all it's cracked up to be?"

"The old guard doesn't love my line of work," Clare shrugged, brushing her black hair back out of her eyes on the screen. "Religion still battles with science a little bit here, but Aleki and Stella are on board and it's not like Manu and I live on the island. They've got a while to get used to it before we tie the knot anyway."

"How is wedding planning going?"

Clare snorted. "Who knows? Stella's barely out of labour and she's already talking about it. She can do whatever she wants. As long as Manu shows up, I'll be a happy woman." She paused, before adding generously. "You too, of course. But not for the same reasons."

"Of course." Clare had asked him to be her best man shortly after the proposal, but had yet to exactly determine what that meant. Again, nerves crept over his skin at the idea of Clare's wedding and seeing Ana there. He'd be hard pushed to write off their London meeting as accidental then. Good thing he had nine months before the September wedding to come up with a story. He chatted with Clare a little longer before signing off, but the anxiety clung to him as the screen went black.

You don't make things easy on yourself, Miller.

Oliana Maiava might be one of the biggest surprises of his thirty years on the planet. He couldn't wait to see her again.

FIVE

Thunk!

Ana sighed as she crouched down to pick up the book she'd dropped. The wet slap of rain against the shop window provided a gloomy soundtrack that seemed fitting as she shelved new copies of another billionaire tech bro's memoir.

"Why do we stock this shit, Gert?" she called towards the front of the store. "These guys could solve half the world's problems with their wealth and instead they fritter it away on space tourism and divorce lawyers. Aren't we encouraging them by selling their books to the unsuspecting public?"

"We are. But I'm making money off them too. The least the useless gits can do is help small business owners like me turn a profit while they're gallivanting around the heavens with their oddly named children."

Ana brushed off her hands and headed back up to the counter where the piles of new stock sat, waiting to be shelved. "Have you got kids, Gert?"

"One boy. Lives in Cairo with his Australian wife. They're teachers at one of those international schools."

"Do you miss him?"

Gert shrugged. "I do. His work flies him back once a year and I get to spend a couple of weeks with him and my grandson."

Ana smiled at the thought of Gert in a grandmotherly role. Freshly iced biscuits and hand-knitted jumpers didn't seem her style. "How old is he?"

"Twelve. He hooked up my computer last time he was here, so we can play video games online together." Gert's face twisted in a wry grin. "I'm sure he takes a few hits on the battlefield for me, but he hasn't said anything yet, bless him."

That's more like it.

"What about you, love? Any grandparents?"

Ana's shoulders tightened as she lifted a short tower of middle grade books and headed to the far wall to slot them into place amongst the brightly coloured spines.

"Nope." Maybe if her grandparents had been alive, her life would have gone in a different direction. Perhaps they would have stepped in and taken her, or stopped her from being given to her maternal aunt and her husband to raise.

"What about your parents?"

Ana threw a startled look over her shoulder and Gert threw her wizened hands in the air. "Ah, come on now, love. It's clear as day you're hiding from someone. I'm not going to turn you in. I'm only making conversation. Though," the older lady intoned thoughtfully, "I would appreciate a heads-up if you've got an abusive husband or someone looking for you. Barry's getting old. He might not have the power he used to."

"Barry?"

Gert disappeared downwards for a second, then straightened, plonking a wooden softball bat scarred with ink and scratches onto the counter where she sold elegant middle-class women their interior decorating magazines and kinky romance novels. "Barry the Bat," she declared. "He's still got a bit of heft to him, but it's good to know in advance if he's likely to be needed. Truth be told," the elderly woman confided, "my shoulder mobility isn't what it was when I played. I might need to start a round of magnesium if I'm going to be busting some useless man's cranium all over the stairs to your flat."

Ana rolled her lips inward to prevent the laugh bubbling inside her from spilling out. "Ah, no. No abusive ex. Or any ex, really. Barry can enjoy his retirement in peace."

Gert shot her a suspicious glance. "If you say so."

"I do," Ana said. Seeing Gert wasn't appeased, she tacked on, "I'm running away from my responsibilities a little bit. Isn't that something people do in their early twenties?"

Gert shrugged. "I spent most of my twenties lying drunk in various festival fields around the North, so I can't quite recall."

Ana couldn't quite hide her delight. "Gert, were you a *hippie?*"

"'Course I was," Gert snorted. "We all were in the sixties. Mind you," a sly grin crept over her face, "I did bag a Beatle once."

"No!" Ana gasped. "Which one?"

Gert waved a hand dismissively. "Ringo, of course. The least impressive."

"I don't know, Gert." Ana said doubtfully. "I think any Beatle is pretty impressive. The closest I've come to shagging a celebrity is when I went to watch one of my cou-*brother's* league games and one of his teammates came up to me afterwards and told me I had great tits."

"Jesus," Gert looked horrified. "No wonder we're selling romance novels like hot crumpets if that's all you young women have to look forward to in the real world."

"Indeed."

They worked in silence for a minute, until Gert broke it. "So. You said you're running away from your responsibilities for a bit. I take it that means I'll need to look for another tenant in the future?"

Ana's spine prickled as she slid a glance towards her employer. "Yes?"

"Hmmm."

"I'm sorry," she cried. "But I really needed a place to stay, and I loved the room and this is the perfect job."

Gert lifted one bird-like shoulder in a shrug. "Renting out a room in Muswell Hill isn't quite the ordeal you think, love. I can take my pick of tenants. Good to know it's serving you a purpose while you're here, but one thing I've learned in my time is that the reasons people have to do things are usually bullshit. If you don't want to go back, don't. What's waiting for you there that you can't find here?"

A royal title. A messed-up family. Answers. "It's not that easy."

"Maybe. Maybe not. I'm not opposed to young girls running off to explore the world, but if you're on a limited timeframe, you might want to make the most of it. It's a long way back from your part of the world if you miss out on something."

The bell above the door sounded, and Ana turned to see

Jorge hovering near the entrance, another bouquet of flowers in his arms.

"More flowers? What have you been up to, hmmm, Ana?"

"Nothing much." *Kissing the hottest man I've ever met on a boat.* Not that she'd heard from him in the last few days.

"They are," Jorge cleared his throat. "They are not for Miss Ana." A blush crept up his neck, reddening his cheeks. "I thought you might like them for the shop. To welcome in the new year."

"Me?" Gert croaked. Barry the Bat was swiftly dispatched underneath the counter again. "Um, yes. Yes, that would be nice, I suppose. A bit of colour to liven the place up."

Jorge flicked a glance around the store, at the sky blue velvet couch, the brightly coloured walls, the hodgepodge of spines that spanned the length of the walls like a rainbow. "Of course, Ms Clifford."

"I'll get a vase then." Gert tottered towards the back and Ana was delighted to see her cheeks were as pink as Jorge's. She slid back towards religious memoirs in order to provide a sense of privacy, since she could hardly go sprinting around the counter and up to her flat without disrupting the delicate atmosphere. Ducking down to straighten the perfectly straight books on the bottom shelf, she let herself think about Gert's words. What did she have to go back to in Avali? *The title?* She'd never wanted it, and despite the princess lessons she'd been undergoing since learning of her true heritage in October, she still didn't know what to do with it. *Her family?* They'd lied to her since she was born. If Aleki hadn't discovered the truth and told her, she'd still be none the wiser. Even thinking about the moment she found out was painful. She and her parents had been invited to the palace. She'd been before of course, but usually for formal occasions or celebrations such as Easter and Christmas. The princes were more than happy to visit their family in the village, sitting politely with their aunt and uncle to discuss family matters and social issues. After that, they'd head to Sio's, where they'd slump on the low slung couch in his *fale* and talk sports and local gossip, inviting Ana to join in with them. She had to hand it to Aleki and Manu, once they'd realised her true parentage they'd revealed it immediately. None of the cloak and dagger secrecy of her parents, biological or otherwise. *Is that really the dynamic I want though?* The role of a sweet little girl they let be a part of their lives, squishing onto a metaphorical cushion on their already crowded couch and hoping for opportunities to say something clever, something that might garner her their attention and affection. No, she was more likely to be brushed out of the way, given roles that built on her part-time work in the preschool and working with the Fred Hollows Foundation to teach reading to those who'd recently had their sight restored by the charity. For the first time, she let her mind consider what it might be like to stay in London. To decorate her flat with something more permanent than the squat coconut-scented candle and Boo Saville print she'd managed to acquire by trawling Camden Market.

Trying hard to distract herself from the temptation to listen in to the murmured conversation at the front of the shop, Ana dug into her pocket for her cellphone, pulling up her message thread with Theo.

Hi.

A pause, then three bubbles. *Hi.*

How are you?

I'm good. And another. *I've been recovering from our night out. I think it might be the best one I've ever had.*

Ana grinned, heat climbing her cheeks. *Me too. What are you up to today?*

Just work. Do you want to hang out?

A shot of jubilation punched through her, her thumb flying over the touchscreen in response. *I'd like that.*

I'll come to you. What time do you finish work?

Three.

See you then.

Sounds good.

Ana locked her phone, her cheeks straining from the size of her grin. *Well, well, well. Maybe Gert won't be the only one with awesome sex stories to look back on when she's old.*

THEO ALMOST SWALLOWED his tongue when Ana sashayed around the counter to greet him a few minutes before three. A pair of dark jeans clung lovingly to her thighs and hips, topped with a cotton candy pink sweater that matched her lips and had a V deep enough to cause his dick to twitch in his pants. He'd known she was beautiful from the beginning - the pictures Alcki had sent through had done nothing to hide her features, but the more he saw her, the more he was exposed to the swing of her hips as she walked, the playful glint in her eyes, the more he understood. London Ana was *sexy*. Whatever illusions the Esera brothers harboured about their little sister's naivety, she clearly wasn't inclined to play to type.

She proved it now, reaching up to press her lips against the curve of his jaw. "It's great to see you."

"You too," he growled. Her eyes widened and he gentled his tone. "You look lovely." *There, see? I'm a safe guy. I'm not going to rip your clothes off and lick you to completion against the counter. More's the pity.*

He waited while she cashed up the till, fetched her hat, gloves and coat, and followed her out into the brisk air, pausing as she locked the bookshop door behind them.

"What do you want to do?"

"Anything," she replied, wrapping her gloved fingers around his. "But I need to eat and I want to do it with a view. I skipped lunch and staring out the little window of my flat while I eat cereal doesn't sound appealing today. I want a little more."

I'd give you anything. Theo swatted the thought away and nodded. "Come on, then." He led her out of the bookshop doorway and down a block to a fancy-looking fish and chip shop. The Chippie was picked out in a faded gold old English style font against a British racing green background. Inside, the air smelled like oil and batter, a rich, heady scent that clung to the walls like tradition. Behind the counter, chefs in white aprons were furiously slicing potatoes and battering fish, while others dropped their work into vats of sizzling golden oil. A robust gentleman with an impressive moustache and Cockney accent took orders while a young Greek woman called numbers and handed over parcels wrapped in faux-newspaper.

"Fish okay?"

"Yes please," she answered and he went to order. When he came back she was reading the brass-framed certificates that lined the wall espousing the shop's dedication to supporting sustainable fishing practices, showcasing achievements. "Look," she said, pointing to a set of framed documents done in a newspaper column style. "Only two families have owned this place in over sixty years." They stood together, arms brushing as they read the story of the families who had earned numerous awards for their take on Britain's classic takeaway. After a quick wait, Theo's number was called and he accepted their own steaming parcels, tucking them under his arm. Following Ana into the brisk afternoon air, he caught her hand and guided her to the left, away from the bookshop.

"Is this alright?"

"Yes." Through their gloves her heat reached the deepest part of him. Or maybe that was his blood - warming up, pumping faster, just by being around her. He couldn't remember ever feeling like this. Maybe when he was younger, when adolescent crushes came hard and fast, dizzying in their intensity. But not since he'd enlisted. There had been time for them, sure. Half of army life was sitting around waiting for something to happen, even in the cybersecurity division, but nobody had captured his interest like this. The closest had been Jeremy, in all his hot ginger lumberjack glory, but once Theo had pulled back to prevent his nightmares from being discovered, that had faded into a comfortable friendship layered over a past of fond memories. Ana, though... Ana with rose gold cheeks in the frigid air, breath puffing out from between pillowy lips. Ana who almost matched him for height and stride length, sauntering alongside him with ridiculously long legs he was dying to see bare again, to feel wrapped around his hips. He could never feel fond of her. Never. His lust, his curiosity, his craving for her; it was too big, too unwieldy to be stuffed into an easy acquaintanceship. Whatever it was, it burned him up inside. The chill of the afternoon was no match for it as they strolled down the rapidly-darkening streets. The streetlamps switched on as they walked, dotting the footpath with yellow halos as they lent their light to pedestrians hurrying home.

"How are you enjoying London?" Theo asked as they walked, the city bustling around them, underscored by the faint tune of sirens.

"I love it," Ana smiled over at him. "I know I haven't seen much yet, but it feels like a whole different world to me. I want to do tourist things at some point too, but being here is an experience in itself."

"What do you like most about it?"

"The anonymity," she answered immediately. "Nobody knows who I am. I don't know who anybody else is, beyond you, Gert, Jorge and a couple of other Muswell Hill people. I've never walked down a street and known nobody. I've never even walked down a street where I didn't look the same as everyone else. It's fascinating."

"Does everyone know you where you come from?"

She hesitated slightly, her fingers tightening around his hand for the barest fraction of a second. "Yeah. Yeah, they do."

"That must be hard."

"It is. I don't think I'm being selfish," she mused, tucking a strand of dark hair behind her ear. "I know this isn't forever. Just a few weeks out of my whole life where I can feel free to be myself, without any eyes on me. That's not too much to ask, is it?" She turned to him, dark eyes huge and bottomless and his throat thickened, guilt reaching up to clutch at his vocal chords.

"No," he croaked. "That's not too much to ask."

"What about you?" She smiled at him guilelessly, and Theo knew he was an absolute shit. "You came here for business?"

"Yeah."

If only she knew having takeaways with her *was* his business. She was likely to murder him. They were at the perfect place for it too, he thought, as he steered her into Highgate Wood. Could be days before anyone discovered him in the sprawling grounds.

They headed along one of the park's paths. The bare trees that lined the sod track stretched above them, stark and pale against the grey sky, branches interlacing like a crown of thorns in places where they grew too close, too wild in the middle of North London's urban development.

"This is amazing," Ana said as they took a seat at a wooden picnic table near the edge of a large green field. The tabletop was weathered silver and smooth to the touch when Theo lay their faux-newsprint parcels on it. Claiming the spot on the bench seat next to her, meaning they could both look out at the grassy expanse, he passed one of the packets to her.

"Real English fish and chips. Let's see what those four generations of chip makers have been up to."

She tore into the packet hungrily. Fortunately, the walk had given their orders time to cool, because the runaway princess of Avali promptly shoved three fat golden chips into her mouth and moaned. Theo's cock twitched in his pants.

"Oh my gods, Theo. These are delicious." She reached for another handful and he opened his own packet, the smell hitting him like a familiar fist, effectively killing his burgeoning erection. Fish and chip Fridays with his nana had been his favourite growing up - sitting on the pink shag rug in front of the fireplace, past generations looking down on him in sepia tones from the mantel as he swirled his chips through the homemade tomato sauce his nana made every autumn with bounty from her greenhouse. Those few short years between the cold emptiness of his mother's custody and the prickly uncertainty of foster care had been his saving grace. He'd clung to those memories as he aged, holding them close, pristine and precious, to his young heart. Once the Millers began the process of adopting him, he'd lied about not liking fish and chips so he wouldn't have to relive a poorer imitation of the ritual without the scent of White Diamonds and the sound of his nana humming Glen Campbell haunting the air.

"How did you find this place?" Ana asked once they'd made a significant dent in their meal.

Theo hesitated before answering. *Fuck it, she'd already seen me have an attack.* "When I moved here I went to most of the larger city's parks and heaths to run. Normally I run on the streets in Clapham because it's convenient, but sometimes," he shrugged, "sometimes I like to forget where I am. Woods like these, they feel like home to me. When I'm running through trees on a dirt track I can pretend I'm back in New Zealand." He hesitated, then pushed forward. "My subconscious calms down when I'm on a trail like this. Stops looking for the danger that comes in the middle of a big city. I can focus on whatever problem I need to think about and I usually manage to finish the run with a solution."

"Interesting." She studied him, before looking across the fields to where a light layer of fog flirted with the green expanse.

"I like to escape too," she said suddenly. "This is the first time I've travelled, but I read a lot. Celebrity magazines," she admitted, an adorable blush climbing her cheeks. "I hide them under my bed like they're porn. I also use my brother's Netflix account, but I put my profile under 'Settings' so he doesn't realise what I'm watching. He hasn't worked it out yet."

Theo's brain short-circuited the moment he heard the word 'porn' come out of her sweet, lush mouth.

"More porn?" He croaked the question out, like a toad with a hard-on.

"No," she grinned down at her packet. "Just a lot of romantic comedies. A few sitcoms. There's a lot of pressure on me to behave in a certain way at home, especially as a daughter. I like to pretend sometimes that I can be the sassy girl with an answer for anything, running off to Aspen for skiing or clubbing in Las Vegas."

"You've been clubbing in London," he pointed out, desperately trying to get his body to behave, to wrestle down the beast of his attraction that was straining at the leash, ready to rise up and rip him to shreds for the taste of her. He searched for a memory that would calm the raging need inside him. *Remember that time in foster care with the Pritchetts when their arsehole son came onto you and when you rejected him, he told his parents you'd stolen his wallet?* He'd only been fourteen for fuck's sake, the other guy was home on his university holidays. The ugly recollection worked, his desire waning to a manageable degree.

"That I have." Ana held one of her chips out towards him and they touched potato batons in a silent cheers. "I don't even talk like this at home," she admitted. "I'm supposed to use proper language at all times to avoid embarrassing my family."

"That sounds like hard work."

"Being a good Pacific daughter *is* hard work."

"The devil works hard, but Ana works harder?"

She laughed, a light teasing sound that wrapped around him like a blanket made of stars. He was gone on her. Absolutely smitten. The realisation should have frightened him, should have had him running for the hills. The dynamics were shite - her family, his job, her family hiring him to make her his job, but he felt free, like the expanse of the universe stretched out in front of him with Ana as the centrepoint. *You want adventure, sweetheart? Call me Indiana Jones. You're my golden idol.*

"What about you?" She bit into her battered cod and chewed, grease painting her lips in the dying light, and Theo wrestled himself back, locking down every instinct that was screaming at him to tell her the truth, sweep her up, take her to bed and ruin himself for life in the sweet curves of her body.

"What about me?" He shoved his own fish into his mouth and took a hearty bite, chewing slowly to buy himself time.

"How hard do you work?" Ana asked, swallowing another mouthful of the flaky fish. "It doesn't seem to be a big deal for you to trek all the way across the city on a weekday in the middle of the afternoon."

"Some things are worth losing an hour of my life to the Northern Line," Theo answered loftily.

"Smooth. But actually?"

Theo shrugged and looked down at his pile of glossy chips, poking them around until he found a crispy one. "Internet-based work is reasonably flexible. I'm currently working for an international client, and any work I send through in the morning is in their inbox when they wake up the next day." None of it was a lie, but the dishonesty of his omission rubbed him like a burr, eating away at the easy rapport he'd found himself falling into with Ana. *Tell her, tell her, tell her*, the traitorous voice in his head whispered, and he shoved it away because hope was a wonderful thing, but delusion was not. He'd have to be deluded to think that Ana would still want to see him after she learned he was merely an employee of her family keeping an eye on her. Even as he cursed himself for the position he was in, he couldn't regret taking the job. Meeting Ana - the real Ana, not the biddable innocent Aleki and Manu thought she was - was a blessing. If they'd met later, they wouldn't be Theo and Ana. No, they'd be Tex and Oliana, drawn together by familial obligations and invisible lines in the sand, not by the push and pull of attraction and liberty in a city both of them had run to in order to find themselves and their purposes.

"So," he said, changing the subject. "What's next on this famous list of yours?"

"The protest," Ana declared firmly. "I need to find one I want to participate in. I figure that will take longer than the tattoo, therefore I need to get onto it first."

Theo snorted. "I think you might be underestimating London. I could find you a dozen protests for tomorrow, but getting a tattoo appointment with a decent artist in this city could take weeks."

Ana's face fell. "Oh. Well, I've almost narrowed down my protests anyway. I've only got a couple of causes to choose between."

"You don't have to stop at one." The words slipped out of Theo's lips before he could stop them. *Shut up!* His brain screamed at him. *The more protests she attends, the more likely she could wind up arrested or in the press. You're hardly going to get paid if that happens.*

"For example," he added hurriedly. "We're protesting right now."

She flashed him a dubious look. "We are?"

"We are. We're protesting the tyranny of forks." He

waggled his fingers at her. "Cutlery is a tool of the upper classes you know, designed to keep us from living our best lives, which as everyone knows is eating fish and chips on a park bench. Also, cutlery is super ableist."

Ana had begun rolling her eyes as soon as he'd mentioned the upper class. "You're a dork," she told him now. "A forking dork," she added, giggling at her own joke and she looked so sweet and clever and pleased with herself that his desire roared back to life inside him and he snagged her hand, pulling her in close and pressing a soft kiss against her lips. He pulled back a little and gazed into her eyes, pools of liquid darkness.

"Is this okay?" The question was a whisper, a secret passing between them in the shadow of the woods. Ana's tongue darted out, licking the soft pink pillows of her lips.

"Yes," she breathed, and he found salvation in her acquiescence.

Their lips met again, a sweet brush, a light lick, then the warm, willing press. He savoured every morsel of Ana he could lap up. She was like the finest wine, the brightest star, a cold shower after a night in the hot desert. The kind of buzz that refreshed you while your mind blurred at the edges and the rest of the world faded into nothing, until it was only you and that moment. *And what a moment.* She tasted like salt and oil and strawberries, a little hint of her lip balm that had survived their feast.

A groan rumbled out of him and he cupped her soft cheeks in his hands angling them to lick in between her lips, into the warm heaven of her mouth, and then she was moving, her hands running up the close cropped sides of his head, pushing aside the beanie he'd been wearing for warmth. The cold hit him, bringing a few of his senses rushing in and he pulled back slowly, dropping kisses onto her lips - *one more, two, three, four* - until they were staring at each other, a mist rapidly building between them in the wake of their unsteady breath.

"I-" Ana licked her lips, and God help him, his gaze went there immediately, as though pulled by an other-worldly force. "I think maybe I should go home."

Disappointment punched low in his gut, but he wrestled a smile onto his face. "Of course."

She reached out, her fingers trailing across the stubble that decorated his jaw and spoke again. "I think maybe you should come with me."

Sweet, holy Jesus, yes.

SIX

Ana's hands shook as she opened the door to her flat. Not from nerves - *well, maybe a little from nerves* - but from desire. Hell, from power. Theo's face had lit up like she'd given him the moon when she invited him back and he'd watched her all the way home with a kind of wary reverence, like he couldn't believe his luck, but wouldn't be surprised if she yanked away the unspoken promise that lingered between them in the air without warning. A woman could get used to being looked at that way.

He loomed behind her on the narrow stairs that led up from the bookshop, waiting with infinite patience as she wrangled the key into the lock, turning it, stepping through the doorway and switching on the light. She turned to face him when he hesitated on the other side of the threshold.

"Would you like to come in?" *Please come in.*

"Are you sure?" His voice was low, rough and she heard the things he didn't say hidden in the slow deliberate timbre of the question.

"Yes." *Yes.*

Whenever she'd pictured this moment, she'd imagined

herself as being nervous, and she was, but not like in her dreams. The difference was Theo, she decided, as he stepped through the doorway, pulling off his beanie as he did. His hazel eyes were dark with heat, the low wattage bulb hanging from the ceiling casting the tips of his short blond hair with light, like a crooked halo. Theo, who sent her flowers and listened when she spoke. Theo, who had planned their New Year's Eve with military precision to make it memorable. Theo, who would turn and walk away right this instant if she changed her mind and not hold it against her. She knew that with a bone-deep certainty, and that more than anything made her reach out her hand and tug him forth into her flat by the front of his thick black coat. He came easily, his hesitance evaporating in the face of her boldness, and wrapped one strong arm around her lower back, moulding their bodies together from their chests to their knees.

They stood like that for a moment, pressed against one another, eyes caressing each other's faces until she realised what was happening. He was waiting for her to make the first move. He'd made it on the boat, and in the park, but they both knew this time was different, knew where it was heading, and he wanted to make sure she was fully on board. A small smile curled her lips and a warm shiver zipped through her at the sight of his answering one.

"Theo?" She said his name solemnly.

"Ana," he replied gravely.

"Can you kiss me, please?"

His eyes sparkled, humour shining through the dark haze of desire. "It would be my pleasure."

It started out slow, a lazy exploration of each other's mouths, of the brief taste of one another they'd shared in the park, but it soon increased, twisting into something heavier, something far more base, and Ana gripped Theo's coat and threw herself over to the kiss. His lips were warm and firm and she was suddenly, exceptionally *glad* that this man was the first she'd kissed in this way. There had been other kisses, stolen pecks here and there behind the church and in the darkest corners of the market, but not a real kiss, the kind she saw in the rom-coms she loved, the kind with *intent* behind it. Even with her limited experience, it was clear that Theo knew exactly what he was doing. Whatever happened between them, she was both intoxicated and relieved that she'd chosen someone so damn *good* at it to partner with. He nipped at her lower lip and she gasped her delight into his mouth, and he twirled them so that when she pressed forward a little bit he stepped back, and then they were moving, a messy seesawing waltz across the floor towards her bed with her in the lead, and that knowledge only made her dizzier, drunk on lust and power.

They made it to the bed, Theo's big hands gripping her hips, lifting and grinding her against the thick ridge of him in a slow, subtle movement. She threw her head back in a silent entreatment and he traced his lips down the column of her neck, and her hips thrust forward on their own as he trailed fire across her skin.

"Jesus, Ana" Theo gasped, raising his lips from her skin. "Don't do that, sweetheart. I'm trying to behave here."

"Don't," she begged.

"What?"

"Don't behave, Theo. I'm desperate to do bad things with you." She unclenched her fingers from the fabric of his coat and moved them inward to the trail of buttons that hid his body from her. She slipped one free and his groan echoed in the corners of her flat.

"You're going to be the death of me, sweetheart."

"Good," Ana murmured, sliding the next button, and the next open. "I'm dying to be with you. Burn with me, Theo."

She slipped one hand around his waist, pulling his sweater up and yanking the soft fabric of his tee free from his jeans until she could touch him - a smooth, warm expanse of skin over muscle. She walked her fingers back across his hip towards his abdomen, stroking the soft trail of hair she found, the ridges of his stomach that worked in short sharp movements as she explored.

"Ana, please," Theo groaned in her ear. "I can't handle you touching me, sweetheart. It's too good."

"Okay," Ana agreed, pulling back, her fingertips lingering on the waistband of his jeans as she stepped back. "You do it then."

"What?" His hair was too short to be mussed, but his eyes were wild and his breathing short as he visibly fought to regain his equilibrium.

Ana perched on the edge of the bed, crossing her ankles demurely in a way her mother would be proud of. In this position, Theo loomed above her, his size magnified and she hid the shiver of desire that travelled through her.

"Undress for me."

He eyed her, those gorgeous hazel eyes suddenly wary. "You're sure?"

"I'm sure, Theo. Get undressed."

He watched her a second longer, before nodding silently as if making up his mind. He took two steps back and slowly shrugged off his coat. It fell to the floor in a dark tumble and without breaking eye contact he crouched, scooped it up and folded it, placing it gently on the bed next to her.

"You couldn't leave it there?" she asked on a shaky laugh.

"Tidiness is next to Godliness, sweetheart." The deep sensual rumble of his voice shot straight to her core, and she squirmed, pressing her thighs together in an unsuccessful attempt to ease the ache between them.

He stripped off his sweater and tee next, both layers gone in one slow movement, his eyes hot on her the entire time. He folded those too, the action taking place over his exposed chest with a careful precision that had her close to screaming. When he laid them down on the bed and stepped back, she held up a hand.

Theo stilled, his hands on his belt buckle. "Stop?"

"Pause," Ana amended. "Just... stay there for a second."

He complied, and she took her time, her gaze trailing down from his angelic face, over the breadth of those incredible shoulders, taking in the way the muscles bunched and flowed down the strong length of his arms. His chest was wide, lightly tanned with a smattering of pale freckles in the expanse above his nipples, which were flat and a sweet dusky pink. That surprised her - she'd never seen a white man's nipples before, had somehow expected they'd be darker. The trail of hair that tunneled from his belly button into his jeans was darker than she'd thought, given the blond of his hair, and between the two were miles and miles of ridged muscle, each section about the size of a family block of chocolate and she was struck with the sudden urge to lick each dip and flat of skin he'd revealed to her. Ana gave herself a moment to indulge in the fantasy - gods, what must that be like, to be able to touch and taste and play with this beautiful specimen of manhood whenever she wanted? - before waving a hand.

"Continue."

A tiny smirk played at the corner of his lips, but he didn't say anything, simply unbuckled his belt and pulled the wide leather strap through the loops of his jeans. He unbuttoned those, his hands stilling as he waited for her to pull her gaze from his hands and back to his face. He quirked an eyebrow and she nodded, breath in her throat, as he slid them down his legs. Ana caught a glimpse of long limbs, the flex of taut muscles and thick thighs before the denim landed next to her and he stood. She took her time, letting her eyes wander up his well-shaped calves, over the thickness of hairy thighs, until she reached the end goal. It was worth the wait. She wished fleetingly that she could snap a picture - the first penis she'd ever seen in the flesh. Flesh that was as generously proportioned as the rest of him, flushed a dark pink and curving upwards. She let her eyes roam freely, over the rude jut of his cock, the deep grooves on each of his hips, up to the dusting of cinnamon freckles on the creamy expanse of his shoulders. She wanted to trace them with her tongue.

He bent slowly, eyes hot on hers, and snagged his jeans from the floor. Without breaking their gaze, he reached into one of the pockets and pulled out a foil square, placing it next to the pile of clothes.

Ana's insides twisted. *This is it.* For all the imagining she'd done, a fine sliver of apprehension embedded itself in her chest. There was no doubt this was a momentous occasion. Sex could be casual, easy, performed with multiple partners, sure. She knew that. But there was a difference between knowing it and standing here on the precipice ready to fling herself over the edge, falling into the one pit of sin her parents would never forgive.

But this isn't about them, a little voice in her brain reminded her. *It's about you. You and Theo. Look at him.*

She looked. *He's not going to hurt you. He's been supportive of everything you've asked. You want this. And you want it with him.*

Letting out a breath she hadn't realised she was holding, Ana relaxed, uncrossing her ankles, one hand reaching out to seek Theo's. They locked fingers, and she tugged him forward.

"Can I?" She asked the question, knowing the answer, and Theo looked like he was in genuine pain when he nodded. The first exploratory brush of her fingers against his erection had his head falling back on a groan, and the raw masculinity of the sound emboldened her. She wrapped her fingers around his length and stroked, marvelling at the feel of him, the dichotomy of soft and hard, the texture carved by veins and skin and the neatly trimmed thatch of hair at his base. She changed her hold, her speed, the tension, and studied his face as she did, the light from the street outside casting his features into sharp relief. She catalogued his sounds, the gasps and groans music to her ears, and stored them away in a mental vault - her private encyclopaedia of Theo Miller's sexual preferences. He let her work him, let her tease and tug, finding out what he liked best by the hitch of his breath and the pump of his hips until she bent her head to brush her lips across the silken rounded tip.

"Ah, ah, ah," Theo chided, gently pulling away. "That's enough of that, sweetheart."

"You don't like it?"

"I like it enough that I almost came all over you imagining it."

Heat crawled up Ana's chest at the image. Gods, that would be... *filthy. Depraved.*

Hot.

Desire corkscrewed down inside her, flaring out, a supernova - hot and bright. Decadent in its audacity, in the way it stole into the crevices of her body and heart, leaving her flush with wanting. Her legs parted in response and his eyes snapped down to her lap as though compelled. He dropped to his knees between her thighs and the sheer sensuality of it, of having this specimen of a man, naked and kneeling, before her while she sat, fully clothed like - well, like royalty - was more arousing than anything else. This was her idea, her domain, control was hers to take, and the beautiful thing was that she didn't even have to demand it. Here, in the dim light of the bedroom, Theo offered it up to her. He gifted it to her, with the soft graze of his fingers along her collarbone, the gentle weight of his hand on her hip.

"I hate this sweater," he murmured into the shadows that stole between them.

"You do?"

"Yeah." The tip of one finger trailed down, tracing the edge of the offending garment's V-neck beneath the open folds of her coat. "Ever since I first saw it, I've been dying to know what's underneath it. I've been half-hard all night imagining what it might be hiding."

"What did you imagine?" She sounded like she'd run a marathon. Gods, she felt like she'd run a marathon, the rhythm of her chest matching her staccato heartbeat.

"Raspberries."

"Pardon?"

"I wondered whether your nipples would be like raspberries. Dark pink and plump, sweet on my tongue. Or darker, the colour of chocolate, tempting me to taste them. Big or small? And the rest of you. How good your curves would feel filling my hands. What does it look like where your waist meets your hips? If you have scars, any beauty spots, any stretch marks. I spent our entire dinner imagining what you looked like under the sweater and hating it for keeping me guessing."

Ana gulped, her mouth dry.

"Maybe you should take it off and find out."

THEO ALMOST SWALLOWED HIS TONGUE. Obviously, he'd figured this was where they were headed, but hearing it out loud robbed him of every suave notion he'd ever had and it was all he could do not to rip her clothes right off her body like a gung-ho medic seeing his first bullet wound.

Carefully, he edged her coat off her shoulders, letting it pool on the bedspread. His fingers lingered at her waist, thumbs brushing the soft fabric of her sweater before sliding underneath, only to encounter another layer. Then another. It was winter in London after all. If he'd been thinking with his big head he should have anticipated the logic of layering but as it was each new barrier only increased his frustration. She was like a sartorial Russian doll and all he wanted was to feel the silk of her bare flesh. He found it eventually, after burrowing through tiers of clothing and a sigh of relief wrenched out of him.

"There you are."

Theo dragged the layers up her body slowly and she raised her arms, helping him work them off her top half, dragging her hat off along the way. Her hair was mussed by the time he plopped them on top of his own clothes - no time for folding now - and that simple element coupled with the sweet vulnerability of her plain cotton bra stunned him.

She was beautiful. No pretence, no artifice. No black lace or red lips, just Ana, gazing at him through thick lashes as he worshipped her.

"You're beautiful," he told her, because it needed to be said, she needed to know he saw her that way, and when she blushed and looked down, he repeated the words. "You're beautiful, Ana."

She looked up at him again and he held her gaze, willing her to see how much he meant it. Catching her bottom lip between her teeth, she reached behind her and fiddled with the back of her bra. It fell into her lap and in an Herculean feat, Theo resisted the urge to look right away, leaning forward instead to kiss her gently. Ana's eyes were closed when he lifted his head, a tiny smile playing at the corners of her mouth and he dropped kisses on her cheek, her shoulders as he moved back slowly to look his fill.

Holy. Shit.

She was perfect.

Delicate collarbones, rounded shoulders. Full breasts, honey coloured and tipped with large brown nipples. Her stomach looked soft, the thick press of her denim waistband cutting off his view and that wouldn't do at all. He reached out and flicked the button open, searching her eyes for consent. "Is this okay?"

She nodded silently, and he moved his hand to her zipper, lowering it and reaching back up to tug on the waistband. Ana lifted her hips, helping him as he worked the stiff jeans down the thick curves of her hips and legs, taking her underwear with them, stopping only to unzip her ankle boots and pull each one off along with her thick wool socks before ridding her of her clothing entirely.

Theo straightened, his hands working across Ana's body, touching and stroking as he took it all in. One hand caressed the side of her breast and she gasped, the exhalation pushing her chest out, the tight points of her nipples a hair's breadth from his face.

Theo's mind went blank. Instinct drove him, had him leaning forward to let the precious tip graze against his lips. Back and forth, back and forth, a slow tortuous shake of his head, rubbing his closed mouth against the plush bud of her breast. He opened his mouth on the next pass, his tongue darting out to taste her and Ana responded by clutching his head and holding it tight to her, restricting his movement in a way that felt perfect, because why would he want to move when he could stay here, between his woman's thighs, lapping at the sweet peak of her? Theo drew the bud into his mouth, sucking in long draws that echoed through his blood into a heavy throb in his balls. Ana's arms tightened around his head and for one glorious moment he imagined suffocating here, overwhelmed by the bounty of her flesh and his own lust.

No. No, that wouldn't do. He hadn't even been inside her yet. There was no way he would take his last breath on Earth, around a mouthful of her, without knowing what it felt like to be inside her. The thought steadied him and he clung to it as he pulled back, stretching up to kiss the plaintive moan out of Ana's mouth.

"I know, sweetheart."

"I want more."

"You'll get it. But it'll feel even better next time."

"How?" Ana pouted and Theo grinned. *Fuck, she's cute.*

"Because next time, I'll be inside you. And when I am, I'll lick and suck you until you're hoarse. I'll use my mouth and my cock at the same time to give you as much pleasure as I can. Does that sound good?"

"Yes."

"Why don't you lie down and I can show you?"

She scooted back on the double bed, laying her head on the pillows and he followed, the give of the mattress heaven on his knees after the cold wooden floor. Not that he was complaining. He'd kneel there for a year if she asked him to, but the first time he made love to Ana Maiava, he wanted it to be in a bed. Theo didn't have time to explore that surprising streak of traditionalism though, because right at that moment Ana spread her legs, and free from the shadows of her seated position earlier, he got his first look at her pussy.

Good Lord, if his heart didn't calm down he would have to raid Liam's stock of benzos on the way home.

He reached for her, wrapping one hand over each thigh, but she surprised him, surging up and hooking her arms under his to pull him forward and on top of her. They landed chest to chest, his legs between hers, and Theo sent up a silent prayer of thanks that his match was six feet tall with unanticipated upper body strength because their bodies fit together like they'd been made for each other.

"I only wanted a taste," he assured her, and Ana kissed him deeply.

"You can have a taste later. I want you now."

Well, if that wasn't him told.

Theo sat back on his knees, snagging the condom from the bedspread beside him, opening it carefully and rolling it on, tip pinched. He settled onto his elbows, face inches from hers. This close, he could see the sweet flush of her kiss-reddened mouth, the thick fan of her lashes as she blinked up at him.

He reached down and lined them up, pausing at her

entrance, the head of his cock resting just inside the velvet perfection of her lips. "Ready?"

"Ready," she confirmed, and he closed his eyes and sank slowly into heaven, sensation racing up his cock, over his torso and up through his brain, drowning him in heady satisfaction.

He felt her seize up the moment he was seated. Eyes flying open, he tried to meet her gaze but her eyes were wild, darting everywhere except him.

"Hey, hey." He rubbed his nose against hers, watching as her eyes fluttered up to his. "It's okay, sweetheart. What is it?"

She blinked at him. "You."

"Me?"

"You're there."

"I'm there?"

"*There.*" She gestured down her body to where they were joined, where the hot, snugness of her wrapped around him, giving him life.

He arched his brow. "You don't want me there? We can stop anytime you want, Ana." It might kill him, but that was a small price to pay for her happiness.

She blew out a breath, frustrated. "It's not that. I mean, I *want* you there. It's just... It's awkward."

"Awkward," Theo repeated, keeping his voice flat.

She nodded slightly, her hair brushing his cheek, the rich scent of coconut and roses making him dizzy. "I want to make sure it's good." Her voice was small, laced with a hint of vulnerability that reached inside him and wrapped around his heart. "I don't really know how to make that happen."

Theo tried to muffle his pained laugh, but it eked out anyway. "Oh, sweetheart. You have no idea, do you?"

Hurt flooded her eyes and she pushed at his chest, but he leant down and captured her lips in a gentle kiss. "No idea how good you feel," he murmured. "No idea how crazy you drive me." The softness of her lips under his was glorious, the hot press of her flesh around his cock, nirvana. "You have no idea that I'd put in hours here between your legs, just to make you feel good. To watch you take the pleasure you deserve." He pulled back a little and she followed, the sweet pink of her lips puffy from their slow seduction."Do you want to stop, sweetheart? Or do you want me to show you how good you make me feel? How good we can feel together?"

Ana nodded, a small whimper escaping her lips, and he tried not to let his triumph show on his face. He couldn't help the swell of pride and possession in his chest, though. He wanted to beat his chest, shout from the rooftops. This gorgeous, intelligent, funny woman wanted him. She wanted him to show her all the ways a man could please a woman, and he was almost giddy with the possibilities. *Focus, Miller. Get your head in it.* The way he was feeling he was likely to blow in a minute and a half, and that wouldn't do at all. He pressed forward a little, and Ana sighed, letting her legs fall open further, the tension seeping out of her as she wound her arms around his neck. Theo let his forehead fall, pressing against the silky column of Ana's neck as he pumped his hips, a slow easy drag backwards, a sweet welcoming press forward.

"This okay, sweetheart?"

"Yes," she gasped, and he smiled into her hair.

"Anything else I can do for you?"

"I think, maybe," she hesitated before the words came tumbling out together. "Couldyoutalktomemore?"

"What's that now?" Theo pressed a kiss behind her ear.

"Could you please talk to me some more?"

"Course I can, sweetheart." He turned his head, capturing her lips in a thorough kiss.

"What do you want to hear?" he asked when he pulled back, his voice a low rasp. "You want to hear about how sublime you feel around me? How snug and wet you are? The perfect home for my cock." He trailed a line of kisses down her neck as he rocked into her. "How I'm the luckiest bastard in the world to be here with you like this?"

"Yeah," Ana gasped, her eyes glazing. "All of that."

A groan left him as her walls fluttered around the thick column of his cock. "God, Ana." He shifted his weight to his right hand, his left one coming up to cup the heavy swell of her breast. He squeezed gently and she whimpered. "Does that feel good, Ana? Be honest, now."

"It's good," she breathed. "I think... maybe... a little more, Theo."

He brushed his thumb back and forth against the tight point of her nipple and she moaned, a raw throaty sound that ripped through him and left him lightheaded.

"You ruin me," he gasped, his thumb moving faster now. Fleeting touches still, but short, fast, dragging the pad of his thumb over the peak of her breast as he canted his hips, a slow slide and drag that sent fire racing up his thighs to pool at the base of his spine. He tilted his hips, changing the angle, and she moaned so he did it again; the same slant, the same rhythm, and she tensed, her plush thighs tightening around his hips, her breath catching in the quiet of the room.

"There, sweetheart?"

Ana nodded mutely, eyes glossy, and he pumped again, again, again and she was coming, a hot clasp that pulled at his flesh, his heart, the corners of his mind. He stilled his hips, buried to the root in her as her inner walls worked him in sweet, greedy clutches, letting her clamp down on every inch of him, as his fingers plucked at her nipple. She gasped, twisting under him, shaking, her back rising off the bed as she arched towards him, her breast in his hand, her pussy surrounding his cock, her voice calling his name as she pulsed in waves under him, around him, through him. He held himself there, a tool for her pleasure as she took it. When she slumped, panting back against the pillows, he moved again, a gentle sawing motion of his hips that increased in speed and fervour as Ana ran her nails over his shoulders, over his biceps, biting into his bunched muscles. She muttered words of endearment, praise, encouragement, twisting her head to pepper kisses against the arm that held his weight. He dropped his left hand down beside her gorgeous face and pounded into her, wild and uninhibited, the molten pressure at the base of his spine spreading, reaching around his hips to the steel rod of his cock. His balls tightened, smacking against the damp curves of her arse in a wet slap-slap-slap, a filthy soundtrack to their passion as Ana reached up and caught his earlobe between her teeth and he roared, the bite of pain cutting through the heavy wave of desire, twisting it into a sharp point that arrowed down his body and poured out of him in thick, sticky waves as he buried his face in her neck and came so hard he blacked out.

SEVEN

The snow came early.

For weeks the weather experts had been predicting that the flakes would hold off until February, but they stole down one night in the last week of January, draping themselves across the trees, settling on the streets, only to be salted and shovelled and stomped over by boots as suburban Londoners complained about the impact on traffic and the indignities of climate change before roaring three streets over in their giant SUVs.

Ana was enchanted. She was out on the Broadway with her coat and boots over her pyjamas seconds after opening the curtains, twirling around in the gentle fall, sticking out her tongue. She tried to scoop a handful into a snowball, but it was too wet and disintegrated into a sad little pile just as Gert hollered for her to come back inside the bookshop lest someone mistake her for a Dickensian street urchin.

She messaged Theo after lighting the fire in the shop's reading area, and he arrived in time for her lunch break. They strolled through the streets, ignoring the grey mush piled in the gutters and searching for the remaining blankets of white hidden in the shadowed pockets of the neighbour-hood while eating warm apple turnovers from Janice's bakery. Theo regaled her with tales of snow days from school in Dunedin before he'd gone to live with his grand-mother and since she had nothing to compare, she told him about the tsunami warning drills they'd practised in school instead. Afterwards they went back to the bookshop and Theo read by the fire while Ana finished up her shift. He offered to walk Gert safely back to her own place around the corner when they closed up, but Jorge stopped by at the same time with a similar intention and Gert told them to go have fun while their knees still could.

After deciding to get dinner out - Ana was fast growing obsessed with trying as many different foods as she could - she locked up and they headed out. The icy blanket beneath their feet reflected the lamplights back up, thrusting the doorways into darker shadows.

"Oh my gosh," Ana gasped, adrenaline rushing through her, as one of the shadows lurched towards them.

Theo responded instantly, shoving her behind his back, facing the shadow, weight balanced low, guard up. Once she regained her balance, Ana shrunk back a few steps, putting some space between herself and any kind of potential violence. She could fight, of course, but only a little. Sio, Aleki and Manu had taught her when they were kids, finding it hilarious taking turns lacing up her gloves and having her compete against them at half-power for ice-cream money. It had stopped as soon as the taro farmer whose patch they trained in told her parents. But this? This was an unknown threat in the dark streets of a huge city and she was suddenly very glad Theo was with her.

The threat stepped further into the light and spoke.

"Have ya got a quid or two spare?"

"Shit," Theo breathed, relaxing his stance immediately. Not all the way. The back of his shoulders were still high and he angled his body to minimise his mass, but enough. He reached into his wallet and pulled out a handful of change for the man.

"Thank you so much," the other man said, gratitude soaking his voice. He stepped forward and Ana caught a glimpse of bright blue eyes, dark hair and an untamed beard. "I appreciate it." He reached out his hand, and Theo paused slightly, looking at the spot where the homeless man's thin wool sweater had ridden up, exposing the inside of a pale wrist and what looked to Ana like the tattoo of a target.

"Squadron?" Theo asked, so quietly Ana was sure she wasn't supposed to overhear.

The man looked down and pulled his sleeve down, covering the mark. "Nine-oh-one."

"Qatar?"

A grimace. "Al Udeid."

"Duration?"

"Four years."

"Action?"

"Some."

Theo nodded as if this exchange made sense and dropped the change into the man's waiting hand. He reached back into his wallet and pulled out several notes. He held them out and they glinted red in the light as the other man eyed them warily.

"Yeah?"

"Yeah."

The stranger accepted them hesitantly, looking down at them for a long moment before shoving them quickly into a small fanny pack strapped around his waist.

"Thank you," he said again, and they all pretended not to hear the choke in his voice.

Theo nodded, turning back towards Ana. The sorrow in his eyes almost buckled her knees, and when he reached for her hand she clutched it, pressing her body as close to his as she could as they walked away.

They ended up at a small pub down the road. For all that it was plonked in the middle of one of the world's largest cities, Muswell Hill had a particular village-like feel to it that was comforting to Ana. The pub was quiet, save for a few old timers as they both ordered pints and grabbed sticky laminated menus to look at once seated. They ducked under low wooden ceiling beams that indicated the place had been built well before women reached Ana's height to reach a cosy booth of worn red velvet next to a window where they could look out at the light film of snow as it fell.

"Roast of the day?" Theo asked after a quick squiz of the options, and Ana nodded. He was gone, leaving a trail of nervous energy behind before she could ask him to check that it wasn't pork roast. Pork for the reminder of home, feasts and special occasions, and she didn't want those reminders here; not tucked away in the dark little corner of a lovely London pub that existed long before her island was a spark in the eye of British colonial seafaring. In the end, she needn't have worried. It was beef, and it arrived on a plate piled high with vegetables and gravy. A puffy golden disc sat on top of it reminding her of fry bread, but when she asked Theo about it, he laughed, relaxing more than he had since they'd walked in.

"That's a Yorkshire pudding."

"*That's* a Yorkshire pudding?" she asked.

"What were you expecting?"

Ana eyed the item incredulously. "I was expecting a Yorkshire pudding to be pudding."

Theo dragged his through the pool of gravy on his plate before taking a bite out of it. His firm jaw worked as he grinned at Ana and she felt the indignity of her denied dessert fantasies fade away. Instead, she soaked in the way he looked, a woolly sweater pulled across his broad chest, the lights of the pub glinting in his short, fair hair, hazel eyes dancing as she picked up her fork. The beef was delicious, as was the Yorkshire pudding when she got her head around it. The roast potatoes were crispy on the outside and fluffy on the inside and she hummed happily as she worked her way through her first proper English roast.

Theo seemed content too, if not distracted. He stared out of the window frequently, and practically jumped on it if it made the slightest noise. The silence didn't bother Ana while they ate, but after they'd scraped up the last forkfuls of gravy-smeared peas - it grated. She sat there, razor blades of discomfort pricking at her skin while he gazed down into the depths of his pint and the silence built around them.

"They called me Tex," he said, suddenly, still not looking at her. "In the Army, that was my name. Short for technical support. They recruited me right out of high school. I was good with computers, with information, finding it, tracking it. My foster sister gave me the name first. She was teasing but it caught on. The army is very insular, everybody is in everybody else's business all the time and the first thing they do is break you down so they can build you back up. Nicknames help with that. In the end I didn't have an identity of my own. I was Tex. I've been Tex for over a decade, and every time I hear the name now my blood runs cold. I shake. I sweat. Sometimes it can trigger a full flashback. You saw one the night of our first date. A different event, but the same result."

He looked at her and her heart broke for him when he whispered.

"What do you do when the sound of your own name traumatises you?"

Ana reached out a hand and he grabbed at it gratefully, wrapping his bigger one around hers and squeezing.

"You tell people to call you something else," she said, and he laughed, low and bitter.

"I don't know if I can," he replied. "The only people who call me by my real name now are you and my adoptive parents."

"Do you like your real name?"

"I like it when you say it." He ran his thumb across the back of her hand. "When I'm with you I can just be Theo. I haven't felt like that in a long time."

"Theo seems like a pretty great guy to be."

He smiled at her, his eyes a little lighter now, and Ana's stomach squeezed in response before he sobered again.

"Not everyone is lucky enough to get out only as broken as I am. That man on the Broadway. He was Royal Air Force. I've known hundreds of guys like him. Any one of us could have ended up in his position when we left. Any of us. The things we do, the stuff we see...The thing with a natural disaster is that it's unpredictable. Quick even, compared to most armed conflicts. They're awful, terrible traumas, but there's something soulless about an ongoing, sustained event where you see the worst in humanity every day. Even harder is when you realise that sometimes it's coming from inside your own house." He paused, looking down at their joined hands. "When you realise that sometimes you're the boogeyman people warn their kids about."

"You're not a boogeyman, Theo."

"Then why do I star in all my own nightmares?"

She didn't have an answer.

They left the pub soon after, carrying a bag with a take-away roast meal, which they left in the doorway next to the sleeping form of the returned Air Force serviceman Theo had spoken to earlier. Once they reached Ana's flat they crawled directly into bed and held each other tight while they drifted off to sleep.

THEY SETTLED into a routine during the next few weeks. Ana worked at the store and Theo worked at home for the most part, chasing up leads Liam sent him for potential accounts. Liam had been thrilled with the contract from the Esera family and decided minor royals were an untapped market. He'd headed straight to Switzerland to charm members of the European aristocracy after a week in London with Theo going over financials. At this stage it looked like their work for that particular set might provide more of a focus on cleaning digital footprints than physical safety. Theo had seen more semi-royal nudes and online gambling receipts in the past month than in his entire life. Most afternoons he headed up to Muswell Hill with his laptop, reading or working by the fire, and he and Ana cooked dinner in her tiny kitchen area before watching a movie cuddled up in bed. She was guiding him through her favourite rom-coms at the moment, waiting until each film ended before diving into the meet-cutes and character development that she loved as candy-coloured credits rolled across the small screen.

They'd barely finished *Just Wright,* and Ana had

launched into a spiel containing the phrase 'one of the most under-rated films of the genre' when Theo's phone rang. Grinning, he ducked under one of Ana's flying arms - she gesticulated when she was excited - sobering quickly when he saw the Avalian caller code on his screen.

Shit.

His stomach dropped. Covering the screen with his hand, he rolled out of bed quickly.

"I've got to take this, sweetheart. I'll be back in a sec, okay?"

"Okay," Ana shrugged, turning back to the screen.

Theo rushed into the bathroom, carefully locking the door behind him before answering the phone.

"Theo Miller."

"Miller. Good." Prince Aleki's voice rang through the receiver and a chill ran through Theo that had nothing to do with the cold ceramic bath edge he'd perched on. "I'm ringing to discuss Oliana's movements in London."

"Of course. Have you been getting my reports?" Theo asked. He sent the reports every week like clockwork. A brief summary of Ana's daily life, omitting his own presence in it. When he excluded that small factor, they were fairly boring reading. Work, upstairs to the apartment, tourist attractions or exploring small neighbourhoods on the weekends after her Saturday shift finished.

"Yes. Please expand on this week's mention of a protest," Aleki responded and Theo relaxed a little. As much as one could, while hiding in the bathroom of the woman he was supposed to be watching from a distance, clad only in his boxer briefs.

"Miss Maiava attended a protest last weekend, showing support for lifting the ban of medical tattooing images on social media. She arrived at the protest at approximately eleven am, and left at approximately two pm," Theo reported, keeping his voice as low as possible and wincing as it echoed in the cold, cramped room. "During that time she ate a picnic lunch and talked with other protesters. The majority were women. Some were topless due to the nature of the protest, exposing their own medical tattooing. Press was present for a short while, but Miss Maiava is not identifiable in any photographs that may have been taken." Because every time the single photographer had trained his camera slightly towards them, Theo had kissed Ana, moving her head to hide her face from the lens.

"What exactly is medical tattooing?" Prince Aleki continued, and Theo cleared his throat, brushing away the memory of Ana's soft lips on his.

"It's a form of tattooing that is medical in nature, such as recreating a realistic looking nipple area on a woman following a mastectomy or shading skin areas on a burn victim." Theo hadn't heard of it until Ana had skipped up to him when he arrived in the bookshop one day holding a flyer in her hand. "Some social media platforms ban the sharing of images, claiming they might be sexual in nature, which prevents a lot of patients from being able to access real pictures of the tattoos to see how they age."

"That sounds acceptable," Aleki said slowly, and Theo rolled his eyes. Apparently Aleki thought his approval somehow validated Ana's decision to stand up against giant social media conglomerates.

"What about socially?" Aleki pressed. "Who is she seeing?"

Distaste slid through Theo like a blade. "She spends most of her time with her employer, and has made casual acquaintances with other local business owners and employees. I haven't seen her with anyone else socially."

The ambiguity of his statement sat heavy in his gut and he clung onto the fact that the money the Eseras were paying would set up Spire Security - and Theo - in a way that meant he would never again need to worry about how he was going to get by. He'd never be reliant on another person or the government for his financial security again.

"She will need to return home soon," Aleki intoned over the phone. "If necessary, will you be available to escort her to the airport and ensure she boards the appropriate plane?"

"If she is willing," Theo said firmly. "I have been clear that I will not be complicit in transporting her anywhere against her will."

"Of course," Aleki replied airily.

"Fine. Yes." Theo hesitated, the question trying to climb out of his throat. He gave into it. "When do you anticipate Miss Maiava will be returning to Avali?"

"Within the next fortnight would be ideal," Aleki responded, and Theo's heart sank. There it was. The deadline he'd been dreading.

"That's not all," Aleki continued. "Our neighbours, the Cook Islands, recently found themselves dealing with some concerning cyber threats. I've passed along your contact information to their Prime Minister's office. I hope that's alright."

"Fine," Theo said faintly. "Yeah, that would be fine. Great, even."

He finished up the call with Aleki soon after, and stayed sitting on the bathtub edge a little while longer, staring down at the grey linoleum floor, running scenarios in his head. There was no way he was coming out of this unscathed, not with Clare and Manu's wedding in September barrelling towards them - he was Clare's best man for God's sake - but maybe in the next fortnight there would be a way to mitigate the fallout. Some way to prove to Ana that his feelings for her were real. Some way he could keep her and his future safe with him.

"Theo?" There was a knock at the door. "Are you okay?"

He stood, crossing the tiny room in a single step, and opening the door. Ana stood there, her big brown eyes shining up at him from her sweet, open face. She'd wrapped the red blanket from her bed around her and when she stepped into his embrace he ran his hands across the fuzzy fabric, stroking his hands over it and breathing in her coconut and rose scent until his heart settled and the tiptoe of anxiety across his skin faded away.

"I've had an idea," Ana said eventually.

"Hmmm?" Theo lifted his head from the soft press of her hair.

"I think the next protest I go to will be about mental health support for returned service people."

Theo didn't say anything, his mind working through her words.

"What do you think?" He'd never heard Ana this uncertain, and he sighed.

"I think the fact you want to help is incredible," he said honestly. "There's a huge need for it. But," he tucked a finger under her chin and lifted it until their eyes met. "Selfishly, I don't know if I want you knowing more about my PTSD. It's hard enough for me to know you've seen me during a panic attack. I'm afraid that if you learn more about it, it might affect how you see me. That you'll stop seeing me as Theo and start seeing me as a collection of symptoms."

"That will never happen," she assured him with the naivety of someone who had never had ongoing close contact with anyone who was mentally ill, and he hated himself for that thought.

Ana moved to the kitchen and flicked the kettle on, reaching up into the cupboard to pull down two boxes of tea - normal for her and green for Theo - and it hit him suddenly how integrated he'd become in her world in the short time they'd known each other. He watched her as she moved around the flat's kitchen, putting their cups together and arranging them on the small coffee table by the couch. She motioned for him to sit, and snuggled next to him, spreading the blanket until it covered them both.

"It's not only you, you know." Her voice was quiet in the still night air. "I can't stop thinking about the man we saw sleeping on the street."

"Perry," Theo said. "His name is Perry."

He felt her eyes on his face. "You went back?"

He nodded, eyes locked on his tea. "Most days when I come up here. I offered to pay for a hostel a couple of weeks ago but he got offended and disappeared for a few days. He's back again now, but I don't want to upset him again. He likes Janice's passionfruit marshmallow slice."

"That slice is incredible." Ana sighed in agreement.

"It is." He slung his arm around her and pressed a kiss to her forehead. "Let's change the subject, sweetheart. This one isn't too good for me if I want to sleep tonight." He'd had a few nightmares while staying over, but he did his best to prevent exposing Ana to them - taking sleeping pills, lying on a towel to stop his sweat from soaking the sheets. She always fell asleep before him and woke up later, which gave him the opportunity to hide some of the evidence of his night terrors. Every so often he awoke to find her watching him with concern and she stroked his back while he came down, shivering in the cold air and red-hot memories.

"Let's go to Camden tomorrow," he continued. "After your shift. There's a tattoo shop there that has really good reviews. You can book an appointment." Somehow, knowing Ana's time was coming to an end made him more determined to help her complete her list. They'd had plenty of time to check things off, but Theo had fallen head first into Ana's enthusiasm for her new city, and somehow they'd become distracted from the list in favour of being tourists. Now, though... Now that a deadline had been roughly established, it was time to make sure she achieved everything she'd set out to do.

"That sounds good," Ana yawned.

"Have you decided what you want yet?"

"Nope. I'll know the one when I see it."

He couldn't disagree. God knew, he felt the same way about her. His life had tipped on its ear the moment he walked through the bookstore door and he was at a loss as to how he was going to right it without something breaking.

"Yeah, sweetheart," he whispered as her breathing evened out. "I know what you mean."

EIGHT

Theo was distracted.

It had been his idea to visit Kew Gardens. Ana had opposed it - the idea of visiting the grounds of Kew Palace set big flapping moths off in her stomach, but when she'd casually mentioned she wasn't interested in the palace he'd assured her there was enough to see that they wouldn't need to go near the building. He'd been correct. Instead they'd lingered in the Japanese gardens and the Davies Alpine House, seeing plants she'd never heard of before. The Great Pagoda was closed for winter, but they visited the King William Temple and sat on one of the benches under the shadow of the huge Mediterranean-style pillars. Patches of snow still lingered in shadowed hollows, glistening in the weak winter sun. They made their way to Palm House, the arched glass walls tunnelling up to pointed ceilings, filling the space with light. Theo stopped inside the entrance of the giant glasshouse to check his phone yet again, and Ana walked ahead on the damp path. The knot of tension that had sat low in her stomach since the moment she boarded the plane in Avali unfurled as she breathed the humidity into her lungs, taking in the lush tropical plants rising high above her; the closest thing to home she'd seen in this city. Familiarity settled into her bones, precious and warm.

"You okay?" Theo joined her as she stared up at a giant palm, tucking his phone into his jacket pocket.

She swallowed, trying to reconcile the comfort the glasshouse brought her with the sense of panic she'd fled her homeland with.

"It's easy to think I don't love my country," she said finally, still regarding the patterns the green spikes of the palm leaves made against the pale backdrop of the glass ceiling. "The way I left, the way going back scares me. But I do. I love it. I just don't want it to be the only thing I've ever known. When I go back, I want it to be a choice, because I've missed it, because I want to be home."

"You are going back then?"

"I don't really have a choice." She glanced at him, smiling, but he was staring straight ahead, jaw clenched.

"Look at this tree," she waved a hand towards a smaller specimen. "It's not native to this area. Yet it flourishes here in this space in a way it would never be able to in its own country. And when it's had its time in the sun, when the species is stronger, it will make its way back and the whole environment will be stronger because of it."

"The *Tahina spectabilis*," Theo read off a small plaque. "A Madagascan palm that lives for approximately fifty years. Flowers once, and dies soon after."

Sounds about right. She didn't say the words aloud, but they lingered in her mind nonetheless. One brief period in which to flourish, after which it was all downhill. As much as she believed that this trip would make her stronger, happier, it would also make it harder for her to assimilate back into life in Avali. The perception of Oliana had been shattered, splintered into sharp fragments the instant they realised she was gone, and as much as her family - *all her family* - might try to piece her back together into the passive, biddable young woman they'd seen her as, the cracks would always be the first thing any of them saw now.

She loved that, loved that her changes, her challenges, were right on the surface now, her shorter hair and her tighter clothes and the red lipstick she would never have worn back home. But whether or not she could adapt back into her old environment, whether or not her old environment could adapt to the new her, still remained to be seen. If not, she feared she might wither away, like the *Tahina spectabilis*.

Theo's phone pinged again, breaking her reverie. He pulled it out, thumbing it open and letting out a soft curse while he read the screen.

"Everything okay?"

He grunted, and irritation niggled at the edges of her mind. It might have been his idea to come here, but he'd barely seen any of it, jumping every time his phone made a noise. It was the first time she'd seen him like this, where his focus was clearly elsewhere, and although she didn't require his attention, it struck her as rude that he'd made a point of inviting her somewhere only to ignore her for the most part.

Ana wandered most of the exhibit by herself, smiling over the recognizable plants in the Pacific section, noting similarities and differences across geographical areas, craning her neck to see the top of the giant bamboo shoots.

She found Theo where she'd left him half an hour later, his thumb flying across his phone's keyboard as he typed something out. She waited for a couple of minutes beside him, but when he didn't look up her frustration boiled over.

"I'm going to go."

"Mmm, yeah, give me a sec. I'll get us an Uber in a minute."

"No." She had to push it out. Years of training in diplomacy stretched across her windpipe, trying to hold the word back, tangle it in delicacy and cushion it in tact.

Theo looked up. "No, what?"

At least he heard it.

"No," Ana stated. "I'm going to go home. Alone."

"Why?" Theo looked so puzzled she almost laughed.

"Theo, you've barely looked at me since we got here. If you need to work, or text, or check your dating apps, that's fine, but I'd rather you told me that than disappear into your phone and ignore me for hours." *Gods, please don't let him be checking dating apps.*

"I'm not... I mean..." He glanced down at his phone again. Ana turned and walked away, the low heel of her Chelsea boots tapping against the damp concrete path.

"Ana! Wait!" He was beside her in a second, his long legs easily keeping time with hers.

"I... look, I'm sorry, okay?" He grasped her hand and the instant electricity that flowed through her was almost enough for her to throw herself into his arms immediately. She stayed strong though. Upright, even. A mammoth effort.

"Hey." Theo waited until she looked at him before continuing. "Look, my place is a lot closer than yours. Let's go there, have a cup of tea and talk, yeah? If you still want to go home after that, I'll call you a car myself."

Her curiosity was piqued. She'd never been to Theo's place before. All she knew was that it was in Clapham and he lived by himself.

"Fine," she relented, and his eyes lit slowly like a sunrise.

"Thank you." He squeezed her hand, and together they wandered out of the glasshouse and made their way to the bus stop. They were quiet on the way to Theo's, as they changed buses, alighting finally at Clapham Common. Theo led the way through rows of brown-bricked buildings and shops to his block of flats. The elevator smelled like urine, but Theo's flat was clean and modern, with shiny wooden floors, white walls, a tiny, cramped living room with an exposed radiator and a view out over bare trees and the backyards of row houses.

He made tea, ripping open a new box of black tea bags that she knew he didn't drink himself.

"Did you buy that tea for me?"

"Yes."

When their drinks were ready, they moved to the lumpy navy sofa and sat. Ana wrapped her hands around her steaming cup and waited. She was making a concession being here. She wasn't going to ease Theo in with conversational gymnastics as well.

"My mother is an addict," he said, eventually, staring into the murky depths of his own mug. "I haven't seen her since I was five. It didn't take long once I started school for the teachers to notice things weren't right at home. My clothes were dirty, I didn't always have lunch. My mother missed a few pickups. They called in outside services and I was sent to live with my nana in Auckland." A brief smile lit his face, the edges of it creeping into his profile as she watched him. "Nana was the best. I was with her until I was thirteen and she passed away. Cancer. It was very sudden. We hadn't heard from my mother in years. They stuck me into the system - a foster family called the Pritchetts at first, and after that to the Millers. They adopted me when I was fifteen."

Her heart clutched. He was adopted too. But...

"Why are you telling me this?"

He looked up at her and the defeat in his eyes caused an ache in her chest.

"Because it made me who I am. I couldn't control anything in my life before I turned eighteen. As soon as I could, I joined the army, which meant my life was controlled, but not under my control. I've been distracted by work today, and I'm sorry, but I need you to understand why. This job, my business, and its success is essential to me. With success comes money, comes freedom. I won't need to rely on anyone else. That level of security," he hesitated slightly. "It's very appealing to me. It's what I've worked towards my entire adult life. I don't have anything else. I sold my flat in Auckland for capital. I'm only renting this place."

"All of that is fine, Theo," Ana reached out, laying a palm on his arm. "I understand. I'm only saying, if you need to work, let me know. You don't need to babysit me if you have other things to do."

A wry grin twisted his lips. "That's the thing, sweetheart. I want to be with you. Even when I get a thousand messages from my business partner and work goes nuts, being with you makes it better. I'm sorry I didn't make that clear. It's important to me to feel I'm in control of my life, like I'm reaching my goal, but those are my issues and you shouldn't have to sit there and deal with them by proxy."

"So..." She let her voice trail off.

"So I want to apologise. Today, I let my need for success intrude on spending time with you. I've messaged my business partner and told him I'll catch up with him tomorrow and we can go over everything then. If you want to, I'd really like you to stay." Theo swallowed, his Adam's apple bobbing. "You're welcome to go home, of course, but I hope you don't. I'd like to show you some of my neighbourhood, take you out for dinner, make up for ignoring you earlier."

In the end she stayed. They spent the afternoon wandering through shops almost identical to the ones in Muswell Hill, but a tingle ran through Ana at the slice of himself Theo was showing her. *That's where Theo buys his groceries. That's the Tube stop Theo uses to come visit me. This is where Theo eats alone, joking with the staff.* The last one was at an Ethiopian restaurant he had almost shyly asked if they could have dinner at. As soon as he walked through the door, the brass bell tinkling above them, he'd been greeted with cheers and backslaps from the staff. Apparently, he was a regular, and one who was well-liked. They joked about Ana's presence and she laughed along, part of the jokes they made at his expense, turning down faux proposals as staff from busboys to a chef assured her they'd be better husbands than Theo ever could be.

The food came and it was delicious. They ate with their hands - "Another forking protest," Theo smiled at her - using injera bread to sop up spiced lentils and chunky vegetable stews, sipping the honey wine that was brought to the table in a beaker with a long neck. It was the type of meal, the type of company, that assured Ana she was doing the right thing. That coming to London, experiencing life in a way she would never be able to under the close range of royal celebrity, was the best decision she could have made.

As the thought passed through her head, her phone rang. Aleki's name flashed on the screen, and like that, her heart was in her throat. Excusing herself, she made her way to the restaurant door, answering the call as she stepped out onto the street.

"*Malo.*"

"*Malo*, Oliana."

"What do you want, Aleki?"

"I want you to come home." Her eldest brother's voice was gentle, but the thread of authority ran through it nonetheless.

"I don't think so."

"Oliana," the future king of Avali sighed. "I know you are feeling betrayed. Manu and I both agree you're right to be angry. So does Sio. Biology or not, we are your brothers. We love you and we miss you. And now we're asking you to come home and sort this out."

Ana snorted. "You mean you're asking me to come home and play princess for the cameras while Uncle gets on with the unpleasant business of dying."

"That is uncalled for." Her brother's reprimand sent a spiral of shame through Ana. King Tama might be the biological father of both of them, but he'd raised Aleki. His mortality shouldn't be used to score points.

"I'm sorry," she muttered. "And I'm sorry I can't give you what you want, Aleki. You've always been good to me. Who knows if I ever would have known the truth if you and Manu hadn't told me when you found out, but I have to be good to myself now. And that means I'm not ready to come home yet."

"Oliana-"

"Goodbye Aleki."

She ended the call and wrapped her arms around her body, holding the fragile pieces of herself together before they could be whisked away on the wind.

WHATEVER THAT CALL had been about, it had rattled her. It was clear to Theo, even through the glass and the murkiness of the poorly-lit street. Ana's breath misted in front of her and she dragged in deep breaths, her chest expanding and sinking in a rapid pattern. *Shit.* Too rapid. He knew the signs all too well.

He threw some cash on the table and was on the street in an instant.

Her hands trembled. He grasped them, linking their fingers, and looked into her eyes.

"You okay?"

She shook her head and Theo nodded, exhaling the tremor of panic that pulsed in him at not being able to keep the demons in her head or on the phone at bay. "Okay, sweetheart. It's okay to not be okay. What do you need?"

"Water," she whispered, huge dark eyes looking up at him, fathomless. "I need water."

"To drink?"

She shook her head.

"The Thames?"

"Water I can swim in."

"Not the Thames."

Slinging an arm around her, he directed her towards the street. He pulled out his phone to order an Uber just as a black cab rounded the corner. Theo threw his arm in the air and steered Ana towards it, one hand running up and down the length of her arm. Even through her coat and the fine wool of her jumper, he felt the tension in her muscles, the way she held herself taut.

"Embassy Gardens, thanks," he directed the driver. They were there minutes later. One of the reasons Theo rented his flat in Clapham was its proximity to his business partner Liam's luxury apartment complex. He towed Ana out of the car and towards the elevators, nodding at the doorman on his way past. He was a frequent visitor and had carte blanche approval to visit Liam's. He stopped off at his friend's apartment only long enough to grab a couple of towels and then they were in the elevator again, up, up, up, to the leisure centre floor, and out to the pool area.

"Oh my goodness." Ana stared at the pool, a transparent box suspended between the patio area of the building they were currently standing in and the one next door. Beneath it, nothing but air. Theo ignored her words, dropping the towels on a nearby lounger and moving towards her. Kneeling, he lifted one foot, then the other, easing off her boots and giving each foot a little squeeze in his palms as he lowered them to the smooth tiles. He stood and skimmed his hands up her sides, bunching the soft wool as he lifted, and she raised her arms to help him. Down his hands went again, tracing the silvery stretch marks on her hips as he worked her skirt and tights down her legs. There she was. Perfect in the moonlight, her dark skin glowing, clad only in a white lace bra and cotton panties.

"Hop in," Theo murmured.

Ana didn't answer, but threw him a grateful look before she stepped into the pool, easing down the first few steps before she dove under, resurfacing after several metres in a furious freestyle. She cut through the water, sleek and powerful. He sat on one of the loungers and waited. After twenty minutes, she rolled over and floated on her back in the water, the moonlight playing across the curves of her body in her white underwear and the droplets of water on her face, sparkling like diamonds. She rolled her head to the side, catching his eye and he waited while she floated towards him, settling into a seated position on the steps.

"Hey," her voice was soft.

"Hey," he replied. "You okay?"

"I've been better." In the muted lighting of the pool area, he could see shadows in her eyes when she looked at him.

"Anything I can help with?" Guilt slashed at him, a quick fine wound across the surface of his skin as he asked the question he already knew the answer to.

"No," Ana replied with a sigh. "Just family stuff." She looked at him closely, assessingly, before continuing. "There's some pressure on me to return home. My family" - if he hadn't been looking, he mightn't have noticed the way her lip curled at the word- "wants me to come back."

"You don't want to go?"

"Not yet." Ana stared out at the lights of London, the line of her jaw firm. "There are still things I want to achieve on my own before I go back."

"Ah, the infamous list," Theo teased lightly and she sent him a small grin in return before turning serious.

"Can you help me finish it, Theo? I really don't want to leave London and feel like I didn't make the most of my time here."

Tenderness pinged in his chest, spreading outwards at the vulnerability etched on her face.

"Of course I can. In fact," he added, standing up, "I can help you knock one thing off it right now."

"You know a twenty four hour tattooist?" Ana joked, but her smile faded as he flicked open the button on his jeans.

"Wha-"

"Skinny dipping was on your list, no?"

"No! I mean, yes it was - but not here!"

Theo looked around the deserted pool area. "Why not here?"

Ana looked scandalised. "The pool is see-through! Anyone could spot us!"

Theo chuckled as he lowered his zip, the sound sawing through the still night air. "Anyone could see us from more than a hundred feet below? Are you aware of a contingent of bionic-eyed mutants in London that nobody else knows about?" Hooking his thumbs into the waistband of his jeans and underwear, he shucked them down his legs and marched towards the water. Bravado or no, standing bare arse naked in an English winter wasn't high on his list of recommended activities. But what Ana wanted, Ana got. Even if he had to give her a little push to get there.

She squawked a little as he passed her on the pool stairs, dropping his body down to cover his shoulders in the heated water, the combination of the brisk chill of the air and the comforting warmth of the water a glorious sensation. Glancing back, he saw her still gaping at him and he grinned.

"Come on, sweetheart. Live a little."

Her hands moved slowly, belying her hesitancy, but they did move, reaching around her back to unclasp her bra, and his dick stirred when she pulled the garment from below the water's surface and it landed with a heavy plop on the tiled pool surround. Her underwear followed and he swallowed hard, wrestling down his desire.

This is about her. About helping her achieve her dreams. Not about you, you horny bastard.

She glided towards him, her body still hidden from view under the water.

"How do you feel?" he asked, his voice low, a secret in the dark.

"Free," she whispered back, and the smile she gave him was a gift, open and pure. He clutched it to his heart, searing the memory there, so he'd be able to pull it out and look at it later when she was gone, and he needed to remember how he felt now, in this moment. Like he could take on the world with a smile like that, given only to him.

"Good." The word spilled out. "I want you to feel like this all the time."

Her smile changed, wistfulness tilting it at the corners. "It's enough to feel it now." She twirled in the water, ripples spreading out from the movement to stroke against him where he stood unmoving. "Thank you."

"Don't thank me," Theo croaked. "You deserve the world. I wish I could give it to you."

"I wish I could take it." Ana ducked under the water. When she resurfaced, she floated against one of the walls, arms folded over the edge as she looked out across the lights of London. "It feels a little like I have it at this moment."

He swam towards her slowly, pushing through the silky water until he was behind her, arms either side of hers, chin on the soft slope of her shoulder, the front of his body pressed to the back of hers. A perfect fit.

"Relax" he whispered in her ear, noting the way she shivered against him. Not a cold shiver... a shiver that belied her desire. "Nobody can see us. Nobody knows what we're doing." He slid one hand over the soft curve of her stomach, slipping it between her legs to cup her. "Nobody knows how hot and sweet you keep this for me." He licked his way up her neck, capturing droplets of water. "Nobody knows that I'd give anything to stay buried between your legs, giving you pleasure until you couldn't take it anymore, until you came screaming on my cock." Ana sighed, the sound rich with lust, and Theo smiled, nuzzling behind her ear.

"I won't though. Not now."

"What?" It sounded like a protest, but the way she was

moving against his hand limited the outrage she could pull off.

"That would be a gift for me, sweetheart. And this? Tonight? It's all for you." He slipped his middle finger into her, curling it to press against the spot inside her that made her whimper. "Take what you need, Ana."

She rocked against him, the sweet slide of her heaven on his finger. Gentle movements that seemed to unintentionally mimic the lap of the water on their bodies. Tranquil. Elemental. The inky night pressed in on them, the lights of the city below scattered out like diamonds on velvet as they moved together, locked in a tender embrace. Theo lowered his lips to the silky column of Ana's throat, feathering kisses over her soft skin as her head fell back against his shoulder and she pressed her temple against his, her breath coming faster.

"Uh-uh." Theo raised his other hand, using his finger and thumb to tilt her head up, directing her gaze forward. "Keep your eyes open, sweetheart. You wanted to see the world. You deserve to see it all."

He added another finger, curling and driving, a deeper, quicker thrust as Ana's moans coloured the night air around them. Pressing the heel of his hand against her clit, he set his teeth against the soft curve of her neck and pulsed his fingers, one, two, three times. She came on the fourth, her muscles clamping around him, holding him tight, milking his digits as her release rolled through her. He wrapped his free arm around her, holding her tight against his chest as her body trembled, her arms drifting off the perspex sides of the pool to float in the water as she leaned back against him, weightless but real. Theo removed his hand gently, lifting it and sucking the taste of her mixed with chlorine off his fingers and Ana smiled up at him dazedly, looking for all the world like she was floating in more ways than one.

Theo guided her lax body back into the middle of the pool, drifting her in a lazy circle, lifting his feet to float on his back beside her, gazing up at the few stars that had wrestled their way through the London smog. Under the water, Ana's hand nudged his and he caught it, linking their fingers together while they stared into the heavens, floating above Earth.

NINE

Theo left their towels with the doorman to be sent out for laundry and they made their way back to Clapham slowly, the dreamlike state of their pool tryst wrapped around them like a secret, tying them together. Ana snuggled against him in the back of the Uber, inhaling the scent of chlorine through his clothes and revelling in the secure weight of his arm around her. His hands lingered on her, gentle touches skimming along her back, alighting on her hip, his breath warm on her neck as he followed her up the stairs to his flat.

They took turns in his small bathroom before sliding into bed together. Their legs tangled under the covers and he tucked her into his arm. Her head slotted into the perfect spot - her cheek resting on the curve of his chest and her temple nuzzled into the dip below his shoulder. Ana sighed happily, contentment a golden glow that she sank into like a warm bath with the gentle rise and fall of Theo's breath.

When she woke, he was sitting in his desk chair, tapping away on his phone, takeaway cups and several white plates on the small area of the desk that wasn't covered in monitors and keyboards and various wires, doing gods knew what.

She didn't speak, simply looked at him, the light from his device casting blue shadows onto the perfect lines of his face in the dim morning light.

He's beautiful.

She felt a pang of pre-emptive loss, before Gert's words trickled back to her.

Why do I have to go home? What's waiting for me there?

"I can hear you thinking." Theo's voice rumbled through the dark, though she hadn't moved and he hadn't lifted his eyes from his screen.

"I'm thinking about how cute you are."

A snort of derision. "Kittens are cute."

"Yes, they are. Come here, kitten."

He looked at her then, hazel eyes flashing in the artificial light. "As much as I'd love to make you purr, how are you feeling this morning?"

Her light mood deflated a little at the reminder of the fear and panic that had gripped her last night. She couldn't regret the outcome - an elevated outdoor orgasm had done wonders as a distraction - but the underlying issue of her family's pressure to return home still lingered in the back of her mind.

"I'm fine."

Theo didn't look convinced, so she tossed him a dazzling smile, the one she used to get reluctant readers onside.

"You're lying, but I'll let it pass if you eat something." He handed her one of the plates. "I wasn't sure what you liked. There's a date scone or one with caramelised onion and herbs." He gestured to the remaining plates on the desk. "I got croissants and a cinnamon scroll, if you like those as well."

Ana stared down at her plate, two scones sliced neatly

in half, with little pats of butter cut into triangles. One of the scones was studded with glossy fat dates, the other laced with fresh herbs and long silky strands of slow cooked onions. The sweet, yeasty scent enveloped her, a faint hint of rosemary underneath.

"You got me breakfast?" *A whole range of breakfast options.*

"Hmmm?" Theo looked up from his phone again, and placed it on the desk. "Yeah. Do you eat breakfast?"

"Yes," Ana said, her voice barely above a whisper. "I love breakfast."

He looked at her oddly, but she busied herself with the scones, selecting the date one first. How could she explain that nobody had made her breakfast in almost two decades? From the time she was in kindergarten, she'd been expected to serve her father and brother their meals and then she ate what was left. Sometimes on Sundays before church, or at Christmas and Easter there were feasts for breakfast, but Ana was always expected to help prepare and serve them. The simple luxury of a handsome man bringing her breakfast in bed was something she'd seen in rom-coms, but never conceived of happening in her own life.

He treated her like... well, like a princess.

She thought about that while she ate her scones. How she'd become so accustomed to putting her own needs second that the smallest gesture on someone else's part had an air of fantasy about it - like she could reach out and pop this moment like a balloon and Theo would disappear into thin air leaving only a memory behind. She'd believe it too. Anything that seemed too good to be true surely was. It was the same way with this whole adventure. Sure, Gert had told her she could stay - that she *should* stay if she wanted to

- but Ana was aware that at any moment her time could be up. Iosefa would know where she was soon, and she'd be dragged back to Avali, kicking and screaming - internally, of course, so as not to cause a scandal - stuffed into a *puletasi* and shoved in front of the world, hibiscus behind one ear and a frozen smile on her face as she played the part of the perfect Poynesian princess for the masses.

I bet they still expect me to serve breakfast when I go back to the village.

She shook the thought out of her head. She knew better now. She deserved to be brought breakfast in bed and there was no way she was settling for less. Shame stole over her as she munched her scone. How had she let such a simple thing be relegated to a celluloid fantasy when it was such a small thing to ask of someone claiming to care for her? Not as an everyday occurrence, but the fact that she was twenty-four and this was her first experience with breakfast in bed was disheartening.

She finished her scones, and the cinnamon roll, while Theo ate the croissant and answered emails. When he finally put his phone down and came to lie with her on the starched navy sheets she noticed the circles under his eyes.

"Rough night?" Ana reached out her arms and he snuggled into her, burying his nose in her neck and inhaling deeply. "Did you just smell me?"

"Mmmm." He did it again. "You smell like me this morning. Did you use my body wash last night?"

"Yes."

"I like it." His tongue danced across her pulse point and she squirmed away from the ticklish sensation, giggling. "You're sexy wearing my scent."

"I like it better on you."

"I like you better on me," he growled and laughter spurted out of her.

"Oh my goodness. Is that how you normally pick up girls?"

He adopted an affronted expression. "What are you talking about? That's gold. That's my never-fail line."

"Really? That works better for you than, 'Did it hurt? When you fell from Heaven?'"

"Oh well, that one's a classic. Can't go past a classic."

"'Do you work at Subway? Because you just gave me a foot-long?'"

Theo's eyes crinkled in humorous distaste. "Oh my god, Ana, that's awful."

"I have three brothers. I know my terrible pickup lines."

"You are full of surprises."

"What's yours?" She dropped a kiss on his head.

"My what?"

"Your worst pickup line. The one that shouldn't have ever worked for you but somehow did."

"Ohhh," Theo grinned, slow and easy. "It was dreadful."

"Tell me."

"Okay." He propped himself up on his elbows and looked down at her. "But you need to remember I was nineteen when I used this, and the shame has haunted me since."

"Tell me, tell me!"

Exhaling, he looked down at the sheet and Ana caught the faint tinge of pink climbing his cheeks before he looked up at her again, eyes deep with sincerity. "What has a hundred teeth and holds back The Incredible Hulk?"

"What?"

"My zipper."

A beat. Then...

"No."

"Yes."

"*No.*"

"Yup."

"That worked?" Ana couldn't believe it.

"I'm afraid so." Theo turned over onto his back, pulling her close. She went, still stunned by the horror of his teenage seduction attempts.

"That poor girl should be ashamed of herself."

"Guy."

"Pardon?" She looked up at Theo, but he was studying the ceiling intently.

"It was a guy. I used it on a guy." She could feel him holding himself still under her head as he said it and it hit her that this was important for him, sharing this part of himself with her.

"Theo..." she trailed off, rolling the scenario over in her mind. "That's even worse," she said finally, and he stiffened further.

"What do you mean?"

"That's a pickup line exclusively for people with penises. Theo -" she sat up, looking down at him in concern. "What if he used it on someone else afterwards? And then *they* used it? What if you're responsible for terrible gamma-radiation-based penis jokes all over the world?"

He laughed, the slow, relaxed chuckle he hardly let out and she grinned, pride suffusing her.

"What about yours?" Theo asked, and the warmth drained out of her.

"My what?"

"What line did you fall for that you shouldn't have?"

"Um," she hesitated before plunging ahead. "A guy told

me he hated my sweater. And I immediately had sex with him."

"He hated... your... oh, come on. I can't be your *worst*."

She dragged her bottom lip through her teeth, the sharp sting of pain distracting her from the enormity of the bomb she was about to drop.

"You're my only."

Everything got very, very quiet.

"Ana," Theo said at last, calm in a way she didn't quite trust. "Were you a virgin when I met you?"

Anxiety roiled in her stomach. "Yes."

He breathed an epithet.

"Theo, it's okay," she hurried to assure him. "I loved it."

He didn't look at her, just stared at the ceiling.

"I could have been gentler, or done -"

"Theo, *stop*."

He looked at her then and the sheen of panic in his eyes was obvious.

"Hey, hey, hey." Ana cupped his jaw. "Why are you freaking out?"

He took a deep breath, held it, expelled. He refocused on her, his hazel gaze clearer now.

"I like to think I stay in control enough to make sure everyone has a good time when I'm having sex. Sometimes I feel like that's not always possible with you." He swallowed and continued roughly. "You turn me on like nothing else. Sometimes I worry I'm fucking you a little hard, saying things that are too dirty. Thinking back on our first time... Ana, I didn't hurt you, did I?"

"No, honey. You didn't hurt me." She dropped a kiss on his puckered brow, waiting until it smoothed out before she continued. "It hurt a little, the way it was always going to, but you were so caring. You've *been* so caring every time.

But you don't have to hold back with me. I *like* the way you talk, the way you make me feel."

"You're sure?" He looked at her, concern etched into his face. "You don't want me to stop anything or do anything different? You don't want to try it other ways?"

"It's been weeks, Theo. We've tried it most ways," Ana grinned at him, before hesitating. "There is one thing, maybe."

"Anything," Theo assured her and she rolled her eyes at his sexual martyrdom.

"I want to try being in control."

He responded immediately. "That sounds incredible."

"It does?" *That's unexpected.* "I know how important it is for you to feel like you can anticipate what's going on. It won't trigger you to let me take the lead?"

"You're incredible," Theo shrugged. "Therefore, anything you want to do to me or want me to do to you sounds perfect."

Her heart warmed at his trust in her. "Okay, then. Take your pants off."

Theo whipped his jeans off in an instant and threw himself onto his back in the middle of the bed with such enthusiasm that laughter burst out of her, loud and unrestrained.

He grinned at her as she crawled up the mattress next to him. "I love your laugh."

"You do?" She swung a leg over his waist, a soft moan escaping his lips as she settled on the hard ridge of his arousal. "Is that all you love?" she joked, smirking down at him as she positioned herself, letting his erection part her lower lips and pressing down, forward and back, riding her clit against his length.

"No," Theo gasped, eyes fixed on where their bodies

were rubbing together, their arousal mingling to reduce any friction as they worked against each other, hot and dirty. A second later, he looked up at her and repeated it.

"No."

Ana slowed, her heartbeat thick and loud in her ears. "No?"

"No," Theo confirmed, hazel eyes steady on her. "Your laugh isn't all I love about you."

She blinked slowly as his meaning registered.

"Do you love other things?" She heard the tremble in her voice but she had to be sure. There could be no misunderstandings here. This was too big, too important to let ambiguity in.

"I love everything about you." Theo clutched her hips, stilling her on his body as he pinned her with his gaze, and for a moment she felt like he was seeing into her soul. Happiness burst inside her, a spark that caught and spread like warm honey through her blood. He loved her. Not her title or position, not what she represented, but the real her - impulsive and unsure as she was.

Still staring into each other's eyes, she leaned forward over him, bracing her hands on either side of his head. He bowed his neck and caught one of her nipples in his mouth, suckling the dark flesh like it was candy. Ana moaned softly, arching her hips. When they came back down, his tip was at her entrance and she revelled in the white hot pleasure of their flesh together before Theo released her breast and gasped, "Condom."

"No." Ana murmured, licking into his mouth, the familiar taste of him a balm.

"What?"

I don't want anything between us. "I'm safe. Are you?"

"Yes, but..." She slid down another inch, taking him into

her and he felt perfect, hot and bare inside her; she almost exploded then and there with desire.

"Pregnancy?" He ground out, *one final attempt to be a good guy, what a sweetheart* before she slipped further down his length.

"Sorted."

"But -"

"Theo." Ana brought one hand to his face, cupping his cheek, running her thumb over the soft curve of his bottom lip. "I trust you. I love you."

That did it. She took all of him then, settling him deep inside her, gasping at the angle, at the *power*. She felt like a goddess, and Theo reacted as if she were, worshipping her with the brush of his hands against her skin, with the scrape of his teeth on her curves, with his cock strong and hard for her to use however she wanted, and the sweet filth he whispered into the air for just the two of them to know. She set the pace and he followed, snapping his hips to help her as she rocked herself higher and higher. When she was close, he licked his thumb and held it against the bundle of nerves above their joining and stroked her until she shuddered and cried out, falling onto him as she soaked him, clinging to him as he drove up into her, until he exploded inside her, messy and real and *hers*.

———

LIAM WAS ALREADY SEATED when Theo arrived at the cafe where they'd arranged to meet. The small suitcase beneath the table told Theo he'd come straight from the airport. Calling your business partner back from Switzerland in order to have a coffee and a chat seemed like a bit of a prickish move, and one Theo was certain they weren't making enough money for yet, but they needed to talk, and yesterday's attempts at communication had been laughable, even before Ana had pointed out he was being a shit boyfriend for spending their whole trip to Kew on his phone.

Boyfriend. He loved the way that sounded. She hadn't said it, but since they loved each other, it seemed fitting. He'd been a boyfriend before, but never Ana's and that thought brought a smile to his face as he slid into the empty chair across from his partner, the high back against the wall so he could watch the door.

"Thanks for the seat," Theo muttered as he sat.

"No problem," Liam waved it off. It was deliberate, of course. Liam had his demons, but they weren't the same as Theo's. He could happily sit anywhere, so he did, leaving the seat with a view of all entrance points free.

Liam Barlow was tall and lanky, with any bulk given to him by the armed forces rather than genetics. He had floppy dark hair, wore suits with skinny pants, and looked like the long-lost brother of Harry Styles. Girls loved him.

"Now," Liam began, leaning forward, pushing his hair back off his forehead. "What the fuck is going on? They want us to work in the Cook Islands? And what's happening with the girl?"

"She has a name," Theo snapped, regretting it immediately.

"Oh, shit." Liam leaned back again, raking his gaze over Theo. "Oh shit. You absolute muppet."

Theo opened his mouth, but the waiter came over. Liam ordered for them; two coffees, two full Englishes, one vegetarian.

"I don't drink coffee," Theo reminded him when the waiter had gone.

"You do today, mate. We've got a situation to unfuck." Liam slid a glass of water towards him. "What were you thinking?"

"It's not like that."

"So you haven't shagged her? You've just got a nice, innocent crush that won't ruin our credibility and piss off the kind of client we've spent the last six months trying to attract?"

Theo pressed his lips into a grim line.

"Yeah, that's what I thought." Their coffees came, and Liam stirred two sugars into each one. He passed a cup to Theo who choked down a sip. It was revolting.

"I love her," he managed, once the vile fluid had violated every inch of his oesophagus.

"I don't give a fuck!" Liam whisper-shouted. "Do you know what will happen to our company if word gets out that you're fucking the princess we're supposed to be protecting?" He shook his head. "Of all the horny bastards I could have gone into business with, you seemed like a safe bet. Good old Tex. Same routine every day, doesn't let his emotions get the best of him. Sure, he's a bit messy in the melon, keeps a go-bag in his wardrobe, but don't we all?"

Theo sighed and closed his eyes. Liam could be dramatic sometimes. Better to let him get it out.

Their breakfasts had arrived by the time Liam trailed off.

"You done?" Theo asked, spearing a mushroom with his fork.

Liam flipped him the bird without looking up from pouring Worcestershire sauce onto his eggs.

"I have to tell her."

Liam looked up then, eyes wide with horror. "My Aunt Mary's arse, you do."

"She's going to find out anyway."

"How?"

Theo rolled his eyes. "Her brother is engaged to my best friend, remember? At some point we're going to be in the same room."

"I don't see why," Liam shrugged. "We'll send you to Switzerland and I can be Clare's best mate instead."

"She wouldn't like you."

"Everybody likes me."

"Clare wouldn't."

Liam forked up some bacon, and Theo focused on not inhaling. The smell of cooked meat underscored every explosion he'd been part of during his service. Even if he hadn't been there in person, he'd known as he watched the screens what it smelt like. Sand, sweat, singed fabric, ammonium nitrate... and cooked meat. He swallowed another wretched gulp of coffee to push the memories back.

"I think the best thing to do is tell her privately," he said. "In a controlled environment where she can have all the information presented to her in a logical way."

Liam eyed him as he chewed before swallowing. "You think she'll take it okay?"

"Probably not, but I'm hopeful," Theo shrugged. "I told her I loved her last night, she has to listen at least."

Liam groaned. "You should have done it then. Can't be mad during the 'I love yous'."

"I think you should tell her," Theo continued. "It'll be better coming from someone else. If she realises the company was hired for the work, not me personally it might help."

"Sure," Liam agreed. "Despite the fact I've never seen her, never spoken to the client, didn't see the paperwork before you signed on our behalf. Sure, I'll tell her it wasn't only you."

Theo glared at him, and Liam grinned. "Yeah, alright then. We'll do it tomorrow. So. Love, huh?"

Theo slumped back in his seat. "Yeah."

"What's it like?"

He shook his head. "I don't know how to describe it. Being this happy," he hesitated, "it feels like a trick. I have to work unbearably hard to regulate my feelings these days. I'm constantly focusing on my emotions to make sure I'm not triggered by little things like missing a bus or a cancelled appointment, that something this great tips me over the edge. I feel sick. But like the sickness is golden."

"Sounds great," Liam drawled.

"It is great," Theo argued. "But feeling too much of anything is scary. There's no stability to it. All I ever wanted was stability and this - love - isn't that. It can't be, when it's constantly shifting, always evolving. When every new thing she does gives me another detail to add to it. I can't control it. Not being in control terrifies me." He frowned. "I feel like my mind can't hold it all, that if I let it come spilling out it might overwhelm her and she'll leave me."

Liam was quiet for a minute, pushing his beans around his plate. "I don't know what to tell you, Tex, but if someone talked about me like that, I'd be a happy man. I'll do everything I can tomorrow to make sure she's not mad at you when we tell her."

Relief flowed over Theo. "Thanks, Liam."

A sharp nod. "I've got you."

"Also, it's Theo now." He fought to keep his voice calm. "I don't want to be Tex anymore."

His business partner looked up from his plate, a sly

smile spreading across his face. "Well, okay then." He held out his cup. "To Theo and Oliana."

Theo tapped his own almost-full cup of atrocious coffee against Liam's, the clink of crockery ushering out the era of Tex and heralding in Theo Miller. In the ring of silence that followed he sent out a fervent wish to the universe.

Please let Ana forgive me.

TEN

Blood. There was blood. Drops of it scattered the dusty street like gruesome gumdrops leading to houses, and worse, to smaller things. Pieces of lives, pieces of people, that had been blown out of the streets and the dwellings in the blast. He shut his eyes but that only amplified the sounds. The screams faded, whipped away by the wind that howled through the empty village streets, but they echoed, invading his senses, filling his head as his superior officer yelled at him to get up, to find the next one, to destroy someone else's day and month and life, if they even had one left after he'd been there...

"Theo! Theo!"

He jerked awake, gasping for air, barely noticing when it hit his lungs, free from the hot sand he'd been choking on only a moment ago.

"What?" The word burst out of him and then Ana was there, sweet Ana, climbing onto his lap and wrapping her arms around him. He fought to regulate his breathing as she whispered comfort into his ear and kissed away the sweat that covered his face. She held him until the shaking stopped, and longer. He wrapped his arms around her and clung on like a child, and she stroked the short hairs at the base of his skull like he was one, lending him comfort and security in the repetition of that one small motion. After what felt like hours, she pulled back so she could look him in the eye and he almost wept at the depth and sincerity in her dark liquid gaze.

"Hi," she murmured.

"Hi." *I love you.*

"How are you feeling?"

"Okay." *I love you.*

"You scared me a little there."

"It's a scary thing." *Please don't leave me. I love you.*

"The dreams?"

"And me."

"No, baby." She leaned in and pressed her lips against his, soft and perfect, and the knot in his stomach loosened another inch.

"Never you," she added quietly, her forehead touching his. "I'm never scared of you. I'm scared *for* you. That you're stuck in that place with those memories, and I can't bring you out of it quick enough. That you're suffering and I can't help you."

Theo huffed out the dying approximation of a laugh. "It's not your job to help me."

"Oh, Theo," Ana ran her thumb lightly over his cheekbone. "It's everyone's job to help each other. Don't you see that?" Her words stilled something inside him and a glimmer of hope flickered to life in the darkness. *Maybe,* he thought, pulling her closer and kissing her again, *maybe she'll see my job like that. That I was helping her.*

They sank down into the pillows again, Ana still wrapped around him like a cuddly octopus, and pleasure spread through him as he soaked up the warm press of her body against his; the firm grasp of her palm around the angles of his hip bone, the light whisper of her breath against his chest as she nuzzled into the dip where his shoulder met his pecs. Slowly her breathing deepened, evening out, and she let out a tiny snore.

Theo held her, watching the changing of light as dawn crept across the ceiling, slipping around the cracks in Ana's curtains in fingers of lilac and gold. As the nightmare receded and his heart slowed, he let himself soak in the moment, the simple pleasure of holding the woman he loved.

The brutality of his early life had stripped away much of his optimism that one day he'd find someone who could love him, especially after the trauma of his service settled in, leaking its way out through dreams and flashbacks.

In this moment, he'd never felt so hopeful.

He lay there, weaving fantasies about the adventures they could go on together, until his arm went dead and his bladder could no longer be ignored. Slipping from the bed, he headed to the bathroom, before easing into the kitchenette area to turn the kettle on for a cup of tea. As it boiled, he inspected the mess of her dining table, amusement climbing as he surveyed the tangle of books, receipts, keys and cards spread across the eating area.

Omelettes, he decided. *We can have omelettes when she wakes up.* He'd seen eggs in the refrigerator last night when he'd got up for a drink of water. Quietly, he began clearing the table, moving things slowly into piles. He fished Ana's Oyster card out of the pile and slid it into the small purse she carried her cash in. She didn't have a debit card or a bank account and a tiny slash of guilt weaved in at the determined choice on her part to avoid being found. He fished up a few romance novels, a book on psychology, a popular one on feminism, and stacked them neatly upwards at the back of the table where it met the wall, spines out and arranged by height. He folded her woollen hat and gloves, and placed her headphones on the bundle of wool so they would be easy to find.

The kettle started to boil as he stacked receipts into a neat pile, and picked up the last item, a blue and white striped notebook. He tried to close it properly, but something was wedged inside the front cover. Flipping it open, Theo removed the pink pen that was acting as a placeholder, but paused as the neat script on the page caught his eye.

Final Chance List, it proclaimed in black ink, and he smiled at the line of tidy pink ticks that marched down the page next to different items, declaring almost every one of them complete. The book was almost closed when the last word caught his eye, and he flipped it back open, his heart in his stomach and reread from the top.

1. *Cut hair.*
2. *Stay out all night.*
3. *Attend a protest.*
4. *Go skinny dipping.*
5. *Get a tattoo.*
6. *Lose virginity.*

Lose virginity. Lose virginity. It was right there, innocuous in black ink, but it might as well have been in neon lights for the way the meaning of the words hit him directly in the solar plexus, the checkmark next to it loaded with mockery. Theo's heart stopped, his brain stuttering over the words as they reverberated inside his skull, a slow pulse that grew, blocking out sound and light until all he could see were those two little words and that obnoxious checkmark - *that fucking checkmark* - filling his vision.

His skin felt two sizes too small, cold seeping over the tight casing of his body as the meaning sank in.

He'd been used. All this time he'd worried about Ana finding out he'd been employed by her brothers to watch over her. Instead, here she'd been, making plans to seduce him as part of her Big Girl Adventure Plan. He replayed that night in his mind, searching for signs, and the golden shroud he'd encased the memory in gone, leaving their coupling in stark relief. He examined it in his mind's eye, looking for deliberation, for anything that pointed towards Ana's end goal but all he could see was their wanting, tangled up in the thick weave of lust. Was that it? Had lust blinded him? It sat like a stone in his gut - another way his mind had betrayed him, showing him what he wanted to see rather than the calculation that he now knew had under-pinned the act.

She didn't choose you. You were convenient. Nobody would ever willingly choose you, you broken excuse for a man.

She'd said she loved him. It should count for something but it didn't. Just three empty words, the same ones his mother used to parrot at him before she disappeared again, leaving him cold and alone. Well, look at him now. Still cold, and apparently still alone. *Nobody truly wants you. You're only a distraction before they get on with their own lives.*

"Hey." He looked up from the notebook where her betrayal was listed in her own hand to see Ana moving towards the stove, wrapped only in a sheet. The whistle of the kettle finally penetrated - he'd thought it was the shock ringing in his ears - and she shot him a funny look as she moved it off the burner.

"Are you making tea?" She reached up into a cupboard and brought down two mugs.

"What's this?" His voice sounded like gravel to his ears, but he was too pissed to soften the edges of it.

"What's what?" Ana looked up, and her gaze fell on the notebook he was holding. "Oh."

"Oh?" Rage filled his vision, painting it in thick slashes of red and tearing out of his mouth in the same brutal strokes. "Oh? That's it?"

Ana looked at him, her dark eyes wary. "You knew I had a list."

"You seem to have missed one very important item."

"It had nothing to do with you. Wait," she added, quickly, "I don't mean it like that. I mean," she stumbled, stopped, breathed in deeply. "I didn't tell you about that one because it's *personal*. I didn't want your help with it. I mean, you did help with it, but it wasn't intentional. What we did, it wasn't checking it off the list. It was real."

His laugh spilled out, bitter on his tongue, a twisted semblance of humour. "It was real? Nothing about this is real! This isn't real life for you. You're here on holiday, trying to have a little fun before you go back to your responsibilities on the other side of the world."

"That doesn't mean it's not real!" He heard the desperation in her tone, and the dark part of him that had been pushed aside and left behind at every opportunity in his formative years burst to the surface.

"That's exactly what it means! You think you're going to go home with new hair and some ink and people will treat you differently, but they won't. They'll shake it off as a spoiled girl's attempt at attention seeking and you'll be back where you started, except now they know to keep a closer eye on you. Everything you've done here is an illusion."

"You're not," she moved towards him, hand outstretched, but he flinched away, not willing to let her brand him with her touch. "Theo, every moment I've spent with you has been real. If you believe nothing else, you need to believe that."

"I believe you wanted to check things off your list," he told her. "And that perhaps you weren't especially picky about who you chose to do that with. I guess I was in the right place at the right time. It could have been anyone, right?"

"It was you," she insisted, but he shook his head as she protested. "I wanted it to be *you*."

"Well, you got what you wanted. Good for you. I guess I'm convenient like that." He moved towards the door, realised he was only in boxer briefs and skirted towards the pile of clothes on the chair next to the bed. *Thank God for army training.* He grabbed his jeans.

"You're not *listening* -" Ana started, but a knock at the door interrupted her. Holding a finger up at him in a *stay* gesture, she turned and yanked open the door.

"Gert, I'm -" Her sentence cut off abruptly as a large Pacific Islander stepped through the door.

"*Talofa lava*, Oliana."

"Sio? What are you doing here?"

The other man - one of Ana's brothers - looked her over in her dishevelled state, and turned a fierce stare on Theo. Theo ignored him, pulling on his jeans, shaking fingers fumbling with the button fly.

"What are *you* doing here?"

Ana drew herself up to her full height, which put her eye to eye with her brother. "That's irrelevant."

"Maybe," Sio shrugged, his dark glare still pinned on Theo. "It's time to come home, Oliana. Uncle Tama has been given six weeks to live. Whatever your grievances, and I agree you're right to have them, you need to make peace. The window of opportunity is closing. He will be with the ancestors soon."

Even through his anger, Theo could see Ana's struggle play out across her face.

"How did you find me?" she asked at last, her voice a whisper.

Sio smiled gently. "We've always known where you were. Mr Miller here," he nodded at Theo, whose heart dropped as his sense of self-preservation suddenly kicked into gear, "located you soon after you arrived in London and has been watching you on behalf of the royal family."

And Theo's heart dropped further, because he was well and truly fucked now.

———

"WHAT?" Ana whispered, her throat parched, her head reeling. *No!*

Sio didn't answer, turning instead to Theo. "Thank you for your services, Mr Miller, but Prince Aleki will be ending his contract now that I have arrived to escort my sister home."

"Ana," Theo said, but all she could do was stare at him, their interactions playing through her head one by one, a slideshow awash with deceit.

"All this time?"

He didn't reply, staring at the floor, which was answer enough.

"*All this time?*" Her voice was louder now, louder than

she could ever remember it being, and in a remote corner of her mind she saw Sio look at her in shock. *Well, fuck him. Fuck both of them.*

"You lied to me." Her voice trembled and she hated that, hated showing any sign of weakness, any sign that proved that he'd gotten beneath her skin. She swallowed hard and tried again. "I was a job to you."

"Me?" Theo asked and she almost took a step back at the ice in his voice. "What about you?" He held up her blue striped notebook, waving it around like a lawyer on an American television show. "Were you ever going to tell me I was an item on your to-do list?"

Fury rose in her, blazing through her chest and across her cheeks and if she could have burnt him alive with her eyes she would have. The *nerve* of him to act insulted, when he'd been manipulating her from the moment they met, the moment he'd tracked her down like a disobedient child.

"Oh, but honey, you did me exceptionally." She let every trace of bitterness in her heart colour her voice. "Just like you were paid to, right?"

He faltered then, for a second, and her heart almost broke with it. If there was ever a moment where he could have said something to change her mind... He opened his mouth, but nothing came out. Her spine straightened.

Good. It was better this way, no excuses. He wasn't denying it and she was glad, *viciously* glad because there was nothing he could say that would ever rebuild the trust she'd put in him that was now shattered all over the floor of her tiny apartment. He'd manipulated her, manoeuvred her where he wanted her. Like her parents in Avali. Like Sio was trying to do now, trying to get her to pack up and return home to serve someone else's purpose. To meet someone else's wants.

She didn't *want* to forgive Theo, she realised. She was tired of making excuses for people who didn't love her for her. Every empathetic notion that had ever been drummed into her by her parents dissolved and there was nothing left but furious, glorious anger.

She let poison seep into her smile at the sight of his lowered head. An angel, that's what she'd thought the night they'd made love for the first time. Well, Lucifer had been an angel once, and look how that had turned out. Too bad she'd been so set on her own path toward temptation that she hadn't paid more attention to her guide.

"Don't try and play the victim here, Theo. You tracked me down. You came into my shop. You dated me. And the whole time you were paid for it. Tell me, which of my brothers footed the bill when you fucked me in the Sky Pool?"

"Sweet Jesus, take me away," Sio muttered behind her and she spun on him, her anger celebrating at having not one target but two.

"Shut your damn mouth, Sio Maiava! You hired this man to babysit me, stalked me halfway around the world and came into my home uninvited. I don't want to hear a word out of you."

"For your own good," Sio protested, and the weak thread that'd tethered Ana's emotions snapped like spun sugar.

"It is never for my own good! Never!" She slammed her hands onto the table. "Oliana, do this! Oliana, do that! Nobody ever asks me what I want! It's only ever what makes Mama and Papa look good. It's only ever been so they could shove a crown onto my head and push me onto the family that abandoned me in the first place. Do you know what they said when I told them I wanted to go to university? Do you?"

Sio shook his head, gaze wary.

"They said that going to university was selfish. That I should be humble and focus on my work with the children and volunteering. That Avali didn't need a proud woman in the royal family taking focus from the work of the men and that one day I would understand why." She paused, letting that sink in for her and Sio both. How she'd been held back, her desires pushed aside to prevent her doing anything that would jeopardise her popularity when her true parentage was revealed.

"Did they tell you anything like that, Sio? When you finished your chef's apprenticeship and went to business school? Did anyone suggest you were too proud for wanting to choose your own path in life?"

"No." His tone was sympathetic, but it wasn't enough.

"I didn't think so."

"Oliana, the life of a royal can be difficult. You've seen the problems Aleki and Manu have had. Our parents were only trying to protect you."

"They were protecting themselves, Sio. If they trained me to be meek and mild enough, maybe I wouldn't make a fuss when they told me they'd lied to me my whole life." She could feel the weight of the words as she said them, the truth settling in her bones as heavy as lead. "They wanted to control my behaviour so they could control me. Every-thing was a manipulation. My work, my manners, my hair-styles. They controlled the way people saw me and they tried to control how I saw myself, what I believed I could be on my own. Maybe they didn't mean it cruelly," she added, as Sio opened his mouth to protest. "But it was cruel, all the same. They shouldn't have adopted me if they didn't want *me*. I'm more than my title, but looking back all I can see is Mama and Papa trying to protect their vision of that. It was worth more to them to raise a well-behaved princess than a happy daughter."

"Oliana-"

"You know what hurts the most, Sio? You coming here to order me home? That feels a little like the same thing."

Her brother stepped closer and placed his hand on her shoulder, but she shook it off. Empathy wasn't action. Sio could say all the pretty words in the world but he was still here, doing the royal family's bidding, trying to haul her home to see the dying father who hadn't wanted her. All for the sake of appearances.

"I need you to leave, Sio. Go home to Avali and tell everyone I'll be home in two weeks."

"Uncle Tama-"

"Has six weeks left. You said so." She fixed him with a stare. "I'll come back. I'll do my duty. But I'm not a puppy you can call to heel when it suits you. I've still got things to achieve, and I'm not putting them on pause for a man who gave me away as a baby and ignored me at every family function since. If he dies, he dies."

He nodded, tight lipped. "What about him?" Sio jerked his head towards Theo, who was looking distinctly uncomfortable with the scene playing out in front of him. *Well, good. He can stay uncomfortable.*

"What about him?"

"I can't leave you here alone with him. You're barely covered." He dropped his voice to a whisper. "It's not appropriate."

"Hey -" Theo protested, but Ana waved an arm in his direction and he shut up. *Smart man.*

"How do you think I *got* in this state, Sio?" Her brother

clenched his jaw, and her anger threatened to overtake her frustration again. "Leave, Sio. I'll see you in two weeks."

"I'm not happy about this," he warned.

"I'm not interested in your opinion. Get out of my apartment or I'll describe my sex life to you in detail and scar you for life."

Sio grimaced.

"Two weeks, Oliana. I love you, but I won't let you put this off forever." With that, her brother turned and left, slamming the door behind him.

Ana slumped at the table and buried her head in her hands. The prickle that had been threatening at the back of her eyes since Sio arrived made good on its promise and spilled hot tears onto her cheeks, disappointment and grief mingled in the salty tracks.

"Ana?" Through wet lashes, she saw Theo crouch beside her. "You okay, sweetheart?"

Her heart ripped asunder at his show of compassion. An hour ago she wouldn't have second-guessed it, would have gladly accepted it as another facet of the caring, sweet man she'd been falling for during the last month. But that illusion had been shattered, torn apart at the seams, the ugly reality of their relationship stark in the bleak grey of the morning. She shut her eyes tightly, pressing the heels of her hands over them and gathering her strength, building a fragile shell of armour to don for what was coming next. It didn't need to be perfect, it only needed to exist. Slowly, she took a deep breath in and released it, running her palms down her face and tucking her sheet in closer to her body.

"Get out, Theo."

She might as well have yelled the words for how he reacted, rocking back on his heels as his eyes searched her face. She kept her gaze firmly on his chin, as any connection with those bright hazel orbs and she might very well lose any resolve she'd managed to wrangle into submission. All she wanted was to fall into his arms, to let him kiss away the pain of her confrontation with her brother, but that would be weakness. And Ana Maiava would not be weak ever again. Weakness could be used against you, move you like a pawn in someone else's game. Well, she was tired of being played.

"I said get out!" The scream tore from her throat, jagged and raw, painting the space around them with rage and pain, thick red stripes clinging to the walls, turning her own personal oasis into another prison cell. Hysterical laughter bubbled out of her. Her family had known where she was the entire time. Every adventure she'd thought she'd had with Theo was simply a guided tour of mildly objectionable behaviours cushioned by the presence of a covert chaperone.

"I don't want you here," she said, once her bitter laughter had subsided. "I don't ever want to see you again."

In front of her, still sitting back on his heels, her babysitter clenched his jaw. "I'm not leaving you alone while you're upset."

"She's not alone." Gert stepped through the door Sio had left open, Barry the Bat slung across one hunched shoulder. "And she told you to leave."

Theo huffed out a breath. "You're not going to hit me, Ms Clifford."

"I shouldn't have to." Gert eyed him steadily. "When a lady asks you to leave, you should leave."

Theo's face was a mask of granite. He nodded once, and stood. Through her hot veil of tears, Ana saw him reach towards her, before hesitating and letting his hand drop to his side in a white knuckled fist.

"I'll go," he told her. "But I'll be back tomorrow to check on you."

"Don't bother," Ana said sadly, the tornado of emotions dulling now into a vast emptiness that stretched inside her. "There's nothing for you here anymore."

He left in several long strides across the floor, and Ana slumped across the dining table under the watchful eye of Gert and Barry and cried her eyes out.

ELEVEN

The plane bumped and bounced onto the Bangkok runway, centrifugal force pushing Ana's body against the safety belt slung low across her hips. As they coasted and slowed, a cheer rose from the passengers around her. Ana had always thought the practice rude, but with the lights of the fire engines escorting their plane along the tarmac casting an orange glow through the cabin while rain whipped at the windows, she joined in with the applause. She might not have a ton of experience with flights, but this would surely go down in her limited experience as the worst. Next to her, the elderly gentleman pocketed his rosary and pulled out his phone, no doubt to send a message that he was safe to a loved one. As disembarking proceeded, Ana tidied her seat area and collected her purse, tucking away her pen and checking her passport and documentation were exactly where they should be, on top for easy access.

Despite the late hour, the humidity hit her as soon as she entered the airport. Thank god for chemical straightening, because her new shorter hair would not have handled this elegantly. She made her way through customs, collecting her luggage and making her way to the arrivals hall, searching the crowd of people for a sign bearing her name. She found it, followed its owner and within minutes was seated in the back of a cab, hurtling through the city streets.

She didn't turn her phone on, didn't do anything that might give her location away. Theo could find her easily, she knew that now, but she was hardly going to make it simple for him. He'd show himself when he was ready.

Except he didn't. Not when she settled into her private bedroom in the youth hostel for the night. Not the next morning when she boarded the boat for the tour of the floating market. Not even when she strolled the streets near the hostel alone at night, or ate the best noodles of her life at a roadside table.

After two more days when he didn't show himself, the anticipation started to itch, creeping around the edges of all her Thai experiences like a newly formed scab.

On the fourth day, irritation had her skin pulled tight as she made her way through the streets to the tattoo parlour where she'd made an appointment, while sitting at Heathrow, three cocktails deep. Following the roughly sketched directions she'd procured from the man at the front desk of the hostel, she heard it the instant she turned into the alley. His footstep. It rang out, the familiar weight to it a balm that sang over the rows of parked mopeds and dogs sleeping in the shadows of doorways that soothed her bruised heart.

Well, fuck him if he thinks he can sneak up on me now, right before I get the last thing checked off.

She waited until she was by the rickety door to the tattoo parlour before she turned to confront him, and swallowed, hard, fear coating her tongue when she realised

Theo was nowhere to be seen. There was a big guy behind her alright. White, tall, wide, but without Theo's warm hazel eyes and short hair. This guy's hair was long and lank, his pupils pinpricks in dark eyes.

Every nerve in her body went on alert. But she had to be sure.

"Did Theo send you?" She asked the question casually, slipping a hand inside the pocket of her shorts.

The big man smiled, but there was something wrong about it, about the twist of his mouth and the way it didn't meet his eyes. Still, it could be that Theo had sent someone in his place. Maybe he didn't care enough to check on her himself. If he had, he should know that this guy was a massive creep.

"Yeah," he said, an Australian accent giving his words a nasal edge. He stepped closer and Ana moved backwards, her weight carefully balanced on the balls of her feet. "He wants me to take you to him."

Ana nodded slowly, her mind racing. *Theo didn't send him.* "What's the password?"

The man's face changed immediately. "Now," he growled, the sound animalistic enough it almost startled her out of her defensive stance.

Almost.

He moved towards her, but she darted back, further into the alley, and it gave her the space she needed. She pulled her hand out of her pocket, wrapped around a small travel can of dry shampoo. Twisting the lid off she held it up, nozzle pointing towards her wannabe attacker.

His lips curled back from yellowing teeth in a sneer.

"That won't help you, pretty girl. Give me the bag."

Ana forced down the panic. A robbery. Robbery was

fine, better than the alternatives. Unless the alternatives came after.

"My passport," she managed. "You can have the bag and everything else, but I need my passport."

The man threw a quick look over his shoulder. An elderly Thai woman was turning slowly into the alley, her cane tapping against the cement.

"Fine, yeah. Hurry up."

Slowly, Ana lifted the flap of her cross-body bag, reaching into the depths with her free hand without taking her eyes off the menacing stranger. She'd travelled enough now to know the importance of bag organisation - she knew where every item in her purse was without looking. Her phone was in the front compartment. Her passport in the zippered back compartment. The lighter she had bought from a tourist stall to light candles at temples loose at the bottom. She pulled her hand out again, working as fast as she could to flick the lighter she'd grabbed as she depressed the dry shampoo nozzle.

Fire spewed forth, starting an inch or two from the can and pouring out in a steady stream of orange heat.

"*Fuck*," her would-be attacker gasped, rearing, but Ana followed, arms straight out in front of her, pushing forward until the heat from the flame licked at the man's face.

He stumbled backwards, his shouts echoing off the high cement walls, past the tangled mess of power lines and the lines of colourful washing that flapped in the wind above squat concrete balconies overlooking the alley.

He was almost at the mouth drawing closer to the elderly lady, when Ana slowed her advance with the makeshift blow torch. As he straightened and she caught a glimpse of the shiny red skin that now stretched across his cheekbone and the smell of burning hair filled her nostrils, the old woman lifted her stick and began whacking him across the legs with it, yelling in Thai.

He turned and ran.

Ana hurried to the other woman's side.

"Are you okay?" She had no idea if the elderly lady spoke English or not, but it didn't matter. The woman smiled a wide toothless grin, took Ana's arm and pointed further down the alley. Ana escorted her home, was welcomed in and offered cold water by her son and his wife, who did speak some English, and ate lunch with them. As the time of her tattoo appointment passed, Ana sat on the floor surrounded by three generations of Thai, scooping up sticky rice and sauce with her right hand and watching the little ones practise their dances, their bare feet moving across the dark wood floor as they spun, smiles shining out past the long strands of dark, straight hair that fell across their faces.

After their meal, Ana showed them the hotel stationery her directions had been written on, and the son - Arthit - delivered her safely there on the back of his scooter. It wasn't until she was safely in her hostel room, freshly show-ered and wrapped in a towel sitting on the lumpy mattress, that she processed the events properly, and the truth hit her.

He's not here.

He couldn't be. Theo would never have stood by while someone threatened her. Her bones ached with that knowl-edge. No matter what had happened between them, that wasn't who he was. That meant he wasn't here. She had only been a job, after all. Contract cancelled, he had no reason to follow her. Wrapping her arms around herself, she took deep breaths in through her nose and let them out, the hurt and disappointment threatening like dark clouds, but she clung tight to the memory of today. Of her own self-sufficiency, of the hospitality and compassion she'd been shown by the Thai family who brought her into their home and helped her.

You are braver now. You are stronger, and smarter, and you will get through this betrayal, like you have gotten through the others.

That feeling of warmth and kindness stayed with her for the next three days as she explored temples and markets, wandering through giant multi-storey malls and admiring racks of splendid silks that shone like rainbows, tempting her to reach out and stroke them to prove their tangibility. She caved to the beauty of one, a yellow silk shot through with teal undertones and used the remaining spending money she had left from her work at the bookstore to have it fashioned into a long skirt that was both stunning and comfortable enough to wear for formal events in Avali. As she hung it over the closet door in her small room after the tailor delivered it, the ugly ache of loneliness tugged deep within her. Here she was, thousands of miles from home, having the type of adventures she'd dreamed of, but she felt none of the delight that had sparked through her back in London. She longed for Gert's humour and the cosy book-store couch. For the floral offerings Jorge provided weekly now. Her mouth watered for Janice's pastries and even the miserable weather seemed more appealing in hindsight. More than that, her heart ached remembering how elated she'd been to simply walk the streets with Theo.

But he didn't want you. Not really. He manipulated you. She clung to that thought, repeating the words over and over to herself, letting them build around her heart until the barrier to it was stronger than it had ever been before.

When memories of them curled together in bed, of him smiling at her over his teacup, and shaking on the street after a panic attack threatened her defences, she squeezed them tighter to her heart and tried to believe them with all of her might.

———

"YOU REALLY FUCKED UP, HUH?" Clare plopped a mug of green tea onto the counter in front of Theo. "Just balls-to-the-wall, zero-to-a-hundred, cocked it right up?"

He gave her a sour look over the rim of the steaming cup. "You done?"

"Not yet." His foster sister smiled sunnily at him. "Maybe soon. I'm going to video call Jeremy later and he can rip you to pieces as well."

"Wonderful." His best friend and his friend of former benefits combining, to remind him he was a dickhead who'd driven off the perfect woman, sounded like a peach of a time. Maybe later they could call Liam and he could ream him out for risking the company with his unreliable cock as well. Again.

"What are you going to do about it?"

"Nothing." At Clare's scathing look, he elaborated. "There's nothing to do. She doesn't want to see me. She doesn't want to speak to me."

"That's why you're hiding out here? In Avali. At her brother's house. Because she doesn't want to see you?"

Discomfort pinched in his chest. "I had to deliver my final report to Aleki."

"Sure you did. Never done one of those over email have you?"

"Fine. Maybe I wanted to be around if she changes her mind."

"Aww," Clare smirked at him over her own black coffee. "Look who's a sweet little optimist now."

"Don't you have something better to do than give me shit?"

"Heaps," she confirmed with a nod. "But I do actually feel sorry for you. Even with my crappy social awareness, I can see you're miserable. Where is she now?"

Theo sipped his tea gloomily. "I don't know." He'd gone to the bookshop the next day to talk to her, to sort things out. They'd said they loved each other after all. It couldn't be over like that, but she was gone. Perry, his returned Air Force friend from the streets, had given him a hearty smile from behind the counter, while Gert glared at him from beside her new employee and tenant, holding her softball bat.

"What do you mean you don't know?"

He shrugged. "I don't know. It's killing me, but it's important for her to do this by herself. All she's ever wanted is freedom. I've violated that once, I'm not going to do it again. Not now, not when I know her." *Not when I love her.*

Clare whistled, long and low. "How do you feel knowing she's out there, anywhere in the world, with no backup plan."

"Like I'm going to be sick," he responded, his stomach roiling at the thought.

"Hmmm," Clare eyed him thoughtfully. "How do you think she feels knowing she's out there without you as a backup plan?"

"Probably great," he muttered morosely. "That's what she wanted. Besides," he waved a hand over himself. "Who would want me there for them, anyway?"

"I do." When he looked up at his foster sister, her dark brows were pulled together in a frown. "I'd always want you there for me."

"You don't need me, Clare Bear." Theo reminded her gently. "You're a badass with a fuck off vibe and a mean right hook."

"I'm sure Oliana can look after herself, too."

He flinched, worry pinching at his temples at the reminder that the woman he loved could be walking any street, anywhere in the world, risking everything for her dream of freedom.

"It's not like I'm reliable help," he grumbled. "What if I have a flashback, or a panic attack? I'm a mess."

"Oh, hon." His best friend rounded the counter to hug him, and he breathed in her familiar lemony scent. He'd been scared to see her again, as Theo, to tell her that the Tex she'd known was gone, changed, but she'd barely blinked. "We're all messes. Every one of us. She might be right not to want you around at the moment, but I guarantee it's got nothing to do with that."

"You can't know that," he mumbled, pulling her in closer when she would have moved away. "She's always had to put other people's feelings before her own, and coming back here, that's what she's doing. Even if she forgave me, she'd always be walking on eggshells around me. I don't mind if she pities me. At least that means she cares. But to feel responsible for me?" He shook his head. "I never want that. My brain might never be the same again. I'd just be a burden. What kind of person would love someone they can't trust to be strong for them?"

"That's the stupidest thing I've ever heard." Theo's head shot up as a new voice echoed through the kitchen.

"Hey, baby. Good run?" Clare extracted herself from his hug and breezed towards her fiancé, who bent from his lean against the doorframe to accept her peck on his cheek.

"Yup," Manu Esera replied, his eyes still fixed on Theo, who wished he was feeling well enough to make a crack about the heavily muscled six foot two, rugby league star answering to 'baby'. He wasn't though.

"Why is it stupid?" Theo demanded hotly, aware he sounded like a dick and not caring.

Manu shrugged, moving towards the counter and slipping onto the stool next to his. "Everyone struggles. All the time. Maybe mentally, maybe physically, maybe spiritually. When you're in love it's not about being strong enough to carry the other person, it's about being soft enough for them to lean on. It's an easy mistake to make between the two, but it's important. I lost my best friend in a car accident when I was driving. You think that doesn't haunt me? But when the memories get too loud and the guilt comes, I find Clare. She's never going to make me better. That's not her job. But she gives me a safe space to rest until I'm ready to go back out there again. I like to think I do the same for her." Theo looked at Clare, who nodded, her heart in her eyes as she stared at her future husband.

"We don't talk about this enough," Manu continued. "About how we overcome some of the old ideas about what men do, how they act, their roles in relationships, but it's like training. If you want to get stronger, you have to rest in between sets. You have to train your body to recover the same way you train it to lift or run or swim. It's the same with your mind. Your partner should be like a spotter, who's there to support you, but their main job is to stop you from hurting yourself when you come up against a challenge."

He stood, clapping one huge hand onto Theo's shoulder. "Don't hurt yourself by refusing help when it's there. But don't hurt my baby sister again either. She's been messed around enough by people who claim to care about her. If you want her, you'd better commit."

"Okay," Theo replied faintly, Manu's words still ringing in his head.

"And you'd better make up your mind quickly," Manu added. "She'll be here in about twenty minutes."

The words buzzed around Theo's head, flitting at the edges of his consciousness before landing. "What?" The word dropped out of his mouth, inelegant and heavy.

Manu smirked. "She texted me when she landed at Havalei'i and said she's coming here first. She shouldn't be too far away." The other man ran his gaze over Theo dispassionately. "A shower might not be a bad idea, mate."

Despite the quickest shower he'd had since he left the army, by the time Theo made it downstairs dressed in a pair of chino shorts and a short-sleeved shirt, he could hear Ana's voice in the living room. Inhaling deeply, he stepped through the archway to see her perched on one of Manu's rattan sofas, legs crossed under a long yellow skirt, holding a glass of water as she chatted to Manu and Clare. She looked up and caught sight of him, whatever she was saying trailing off as she stared at him, her mouth a perfect rosebud of surprise.

"Hello," he managed, but it came out sounding reedy. He cleared his throat and tried again. "Did you have a good trip back?" Already his eyes were skimming her, cataloguing her limbs, searching for bruises, marks, hell, for sunburn. She looked great - perfect in fact. A perfect princess, more remote and unobtainable than he'd ever seen her, as her expression morphed into disdain and she turned her attention back towards the others.

"Anyway, I'm not happy about being back, and I'm especially unhappy about being summoned by Sio," she said, effectively dismissing him, as she picked up the thread of the conversation again. "I'll see Un - Tama," she corrected quickly. "Once. I have some questions for him and he owes me answers, but I don't want any pressure from you or Aleki to continue visits after the initial one. If I see him again, it will be my choice and on my terms. Got it?"

"Of course," Manu replied, tilting his head. Theo knew from conversations he'd had with Clare that neither Manu nor Aleki held their father up as much of a parenting role model. That he was clearly willing to stand by his sister and respect her wishes over any demands the monarch might make would have eased his tension somewhat if not for the fact that Ana still wouldn't look at him.

He ran his gaze across her once more, drinking in the details greedily. The thickness of her waist under the fabric of her skirt, the way her black linen tank skimmed her breasts. Her hair, miles from the tightly coiled up-dos and long waves he'd seen on other Avalian women, short and straight and screaming of London and her rebellion there.

Is that me? He wondered tightly. *When she looks back, am I going to blur into a slideshow of her youthful indiscretions?*

He ached inside at the thought. That what he'd accused her of back in her cosy Muswell Hill flat might be true. That she'd lump their time together in with a set of other achievable tasks, wrapped in a pretty box of time and geography, and go on with her life while he sat at home, surrounded by snippets of other people's lives in video and data, crippled by the knowledge that he'd let his pride chase away the only woman he'd ever loved.

He stood there, lurking in the doorway, like a military-grade Lurch, while Ana stood and slung her brightly patterned tote bag over her shoulder, assuring Manu she would stop by the palace and see Tama the next morning. As she moved towards the doorway he stepped forward. She came to a halt directly in front of him, the coconut and rose scent of her hair teasing at his nostrils, urging him to reach out and wrap her in his arms where she belonged.

"Do you need a ride?" Theo croaked, pushing the words out roughly so he could suck in another lungful of her sweet scent.

"No," she assured his chest, and he tried to temper the movement of his pectorals in the hope that she might not notice him actively inhaling her.

"Can...can we talk?" If he could apologise, if he could make her see...

"No."

"I only need a second."

"I've given you all the time you deserve, Mr Miller." Her voice was cold, removed, and an old English teacher's voice echoed in the back of his mind. *The opposite of love is not hate, it is disinterest.*

She looked at him then, and a weight slammed into his chest at the anger simmering in her dark eyes. *That's not disinterest. It's not good, but it's not disinterest.*

"I don't think we have anything to say to each other."

"I do. I have a lot of things-"

"Where was I?" she cut in and he paused, searching her perfect face for a context clue.

"What?"

"Last week, after I left London. Where was I?"

"I don't know," Theo offered. "I didn't look for you."

If anything, her expression grew more hostile. "You didn't look for me?"

"You wanted freedom." He held his hands out at his sides. "I tried to respect your wishes."

"Sure," Ana muttered, glaring furiously at him. "Everyone cares about that *now*."

"You think it was easy for me? I wanted to be with you!"

She raised her chin, viciously smug. "Well, I didn't need you. I did it all by myself. I was mugged in Bangkok, but I fought back and won."

Jesus H. Christ. Everything in him went cold at the idea of his beautiful, soft, sweet Ana fighting off muggers in the Thai capital, but he pushed it aside. She was fine. She hadn't needed him, she'd said as much herself.

"It was never about you needing me, Ana!" The unfamiliar edge of fear made his voice sharp. "It was about trying to give you what you wanted."

Her plush lips twisted sardonically. "Don't let what I want worry you, Theo. Oh, but I forgot, part of your job is meeting my wants, right?"

He went to argue, to *tell* her that he'd give her anything she wanted. He'd build her a palace with his bare hands. *How big, sweetheart?* He'd destroy anyone who'd caused her pain. *They'll never find the bodies.* But over her smooth brown shoulder he saw Clare waving her hand furiously across her throat in a 'cease and desist' motion. The image centred him, brought him back to himself, after the spiralling sensation of being lost in Ana's eyes. They were toe to toe on the tiled floor, voices raised. Nothing about this was right. Not the words, not the tone, not the setting. A groan ripped from his throat and he moved aside, clearing the way for Ana to escape, which she did with one last glare at him.

As the front door slammed and he moved towards the sofa, he felt Clare's incredulous eyes on him.

"Was that supposed to be an apology?"

Dropping onto the plump cushions, Theo inhaled one last lungful of Ana's lingering scent and buried his face in his hands.

"Fuuuuck."

TWELVE

Ana's sandals squeaked on the pale linoleum as she made her way through Havalei'i Hospital. She'd been here before, had her tonsils out when she was nine, driven Manu to the Accident and Emergency department after he sliced his foot open playing league barefoot on the paddock in high school. She'd visited friends and family in various states of health on almost every one of the floors that rose above the noise and fumes of the city streets until the windows showed nothing but sea and sky. The views on the ocean side of the hospital could rival those of the luxury independent hotels that dotted the coastline. But today, as the elevator lifted Ana closer to the heavens, her reflection in the polished steel door looked like that of a woman facing damnation. Her knuckles were white where they clutched the strap of her purse, her brightly patterned sundress wrinkled from twisting the hem in her fingers the whole drive over. All the concealer in the Pacific couldn't hide the shadows under her eyes that painted the story of a restless night. As the door juddered open, the floor number lit up like a warning. Ana closed her eyes briefly and wished, for a single perfect moment, that she had never discovered her true identity. Then she opened them, forced her shoulders down from their position around her ears and strode out of the elevator, projecting a level of confidence she didn't feel.

Her sandals still squeaked. *Damnit.*

She didn't knock when she reached the right door, sweeping in and settling on the bedside chair without so much as a courtesy nod to its royal inhabitant.

"Uncle." She used the Avalian phrase, giving the words a mocking length as they rolled off her tongue.

"Oliana." The king looked terrible, his bronze skin tinged with grey and the lines around his eyes and mouth deeper than the last time she'd seen him, giving him a haggard appearance. Beside him, monitors silently measured the monarch's health in neon. "Please do not call me that. You know better now."

"Why would I call you anything different? You have never been more than an uncle to me, and not a particularly good one at that." When he would protest, she continued. "You hardly spoke to me. I was never invited to join the boys to play at the palace like Sio was. You didn't even have the decency to reveal the truth of my birth to me. Aleki and Manu had to do it. Tell me, what have you done to entitle yourself to anything more than simply the man who married my mother's sister?"

Tama's sigh echoed in the spacious room.

"Has Aleki ever told you how I reacted when he brought Stella back to Avali?"

Okay, we're ignoring me. "No," Ana snapped. "I imagine it was poorly."

"It was," Tama nodded. "I was rude. I was unkind. I was blind to what was happening, and to what I had become in the years since I lost your mother. It took my own son to show me. Tatyana," Tama smiled his late wife's name, the sound lingering on his lips like a kiss. "She was a goddess. Too good for me by far. I was a prince, but I was selfish and lazy. Our marriage was arranged, and she wanted nothing to do with me. I was not accustomed to being denied. Before we had been married a week I knew I was in love with her."

Despite herself, Ana leaned forward in her chair, mention of the mother she would never get the chance to know pulling her in. "Then what?"

"Then I wooed her. For six months straight, I brought her gifts, showered her with jewels, had food sent to her rooms. For her birthday I arranged a private concert with her favourite opera singer in the gardens."

"What did she do?"

"She gave the gifts to charity. Gave the jewellery to the staff. Packed up the food she didn't eat and had it delivered to the poorer villages. She became pen pals with the opera singer and they exchanged letters weekly until she died. That night, the night of her birthday, I was angry. I saw how she had rejected my gifts and my efforts. It felt like a rejection of myself. I shouted." He shrugged. "It shames me, but I did. I told her I loved her and demanded she love me back."

"That seems healthy," Ana muttered under her breath.

"Tatyana laughed at me. She told me needing to be loved was weak. That when I loved myself - respected myself - maybe she would love me too."

"What did you do?"

Tama lifted one rounded shoulder slightly. "I learnt how to work, studied governance and economics, and listened when my father spoke instead of letting myself become distracted. I stopped spending money frivolously. I became the man she deserved, instead of the man who made demands of her."

"Why are you telling me this?"

Tama's brown eyes met hers. "Because I love you."

Ana shook her head, dislodging tears she hadn't noticed. They fell onto her dress, silent drops that spread as they hit cotton. Perfect circles of grief against the joyful fabric.

"When Aleki fell in love with his Stella," the king continued, "I told him love would make him weak. I believed that. I had been weakened by my need for love before. I did not see at the time that he was already a far better man than me, that he did not need his wife. He wanted to deserve her. I was weak and proud when I met your mother. When she was taken from me, giving birth to you, I was furious." He kept his gaze steady on hers, letting her see his sincerity. "Never with you, little one. I was angry with God. Angry with myself. Angry with the doctors and the midwives and every other person on this island who still had someone they loved in their lives. My anger was like poison. It spread throughout me, throughout the people around me. I had no business being around a baby. Without your mother here to make me want to be better, I forgot the lessons she had taught me."

He reached out, his hand huge even in the wake of his illness. Meaty and wide, swollen knuckles and purple veins. Hesitantly, she reached out and took it. From the corner of her eye, the light overhead glinted on the tear that rolled down Tama's cheek.

"I would have ruined you, little one. I was not a good father to the boys. I know that. I was convinced that if I held a part of myself back from them, it would be easier for them when I passed. They would still be able to carry on because they would not have been weakened by their love for me.

Sadness, of course, but not love. You were only supposed to be with your aunt and uncle for a short while. Nobody outside the family knew you existed. The media was not what it is today. I went to pick you up from their house, and I looked at your beautiful face and all I felt was more anger. Anger and heartbreak, because I knew if I took you home, my anger would infect you too. You were too precious to me to spread my rage to." Tama squeezed her hand. "Because I loved you I wanted better for you."

"You never talked to me unless you had to," Ana whispered, the tears falling fast, hot tracks running the length of her cheeks.

"I am ashamed," her father whispered, his own cheeks wet. "I am ashamed of my weakness. Not in love, but in failing to honour your mother with my actions. In failing to honour you with the truth. I said before I was weak and proud when I married your mother, and when I lost her I was weak and ruined. I am a failure in many ways, but never more than in letting you think that I did not love you. I loved you so much that looking at you hurt. After you visited, I would go to my rooms and cry. I would rail to the old gods and ask if there was some way to have you back in my life without damaging our connection further. And I was frightened." His grip was like iron now. "That when you knew, you would never forgive me. You would leave, and it would be like losing your mother all over again."

"I did," Ana whispered and Tama shut his eyes, nodding.

"Yes, little one. You did."

They sat like that, hands clasped, until the sun dipped lower and the room filled with a soft golden light. A nurse wheeled in the dinner cart, breaking the silence, and Tama struggled up in bed. Without thinking, Ana stood and helped him into a sitting position, propping the hard pillows up behind his back.

"I'd better get going."

"Wait." Tama waited until the nurse had left. "Can you please get something from my bag?"

"Sure."

She followed his directions, reaching into the side pocket of the bag that held his possessions, and drawing out a tissue wrapped item. She went to hand it to Tama, but he shook his head.

"That is for you, little one."

Fingers trembling, she unwrapped the small parcel slowly. Inside was a ring; a gold filigree band moulded into traditional Pacific designs, holding a large rectangular ruby surrounded by small diamonds.

"It was your mother's," Tama said, his voice rough. "I have been selfish with her memory for all your life. With your brothers as well. There is a little time before I go to change that, if you are willing, but you should have something tangible as well. Something that reminds you that you were created from love, and that we both loved you - and will love you - until our final breaths on Earth."

Ana left soon after, the ring tucked in her purse. The idea of wearing it felt too raw right now, the concept chafing, but maybe one day soon. One thing she could see now was how anger could twist people into the worst versions of themselves. She still believed her ire at her adoptive parents was justified, but she didn't want to turn out like Tama, holding onto his rage at the expense of his family.

Pulling out her phone, she made the call.

"Mama? Are you and Papa at home? It's time we had a talk."

"TALK TO HIM," Janet Miller hissed, the sound of the boiling kettle doing nothing to camouflage her directive.

Her husband dutifully returned to the dining table with a plate full of biscuits.

"How have you been, son?"

"Good," Theo lied, shoving a gingernut in his mouth and almost breaking a tooth in his haste to become unavailable for casual chatting.

"Is that so?" Ron Miller bit into his own biscuit and Theo could feel the other man's gaze on his face as he chewed. "Because if you don't mind me saying, you look like shit."

"Ron!" Janet gasped, but Theo snorted.

"Well, honestly, Janet, we don't hear from the boy for months at a time and then he shows up on the doorstep this morning with red eyes and a three day scruff. We're not supposed to ask about it?"

"You *ease* into these things!"

"By all means, you ease into it then." Ron grumbled, rolling his eyes.

Janet sat at the table and patted Theo's hand. "It's good to see you, love. How long are you staying for?"

"I don't know yet," Theo fumbled. "I didn't have anywhere else to go." He couldn't stay in Avali, not with Ana having cut him out entirely. He wasn't a masochist, and staying on the island meant seeing Ana. He could hardly avoid her, staying at Clare and Manu's place, and the thought of bumping into her again and seeing the disdain in her beautiful brown eyes filled his stomach with a thick tar-like dread. The wedding in September was going to be torture. He'd sold his central Auckland flat and he couldn't get a flight back to London from Avali. Liam was still pissed off with him anyway, after finding out he'd chased Ana to the other side of the Earth without any notice. Not that it had done him any good.

"Well," Janet smiled cheerfully. "That's the nice thing about home, isn't it? You can stay as long as you like."

"It's not really, though, is it?" Theo spoke the words aloud without thinking. When he looked up, Janet and Ron were both looking at him oddly.

"What do you mean, love?" Janet's voice had changed, a bright artificial tone at odds with the tightening of the skin around her eyes.

Theo shrugged, discomfort pricking at the back of his neck. "It's not really my home, is it? I only lived here for three years."

"Nonsense!" Ron boomed, smacking his hand on the table. He pointed a thick finger at Theo. "You listen to me. You are our son, and we love you. We might have found you later in life, but we chose you and we love you like you were our own. Your mother cries every Christmas you don't come home."

"Ron, stop," Janet whispered, a blush rising in her cheeks as she wiped away a tear.

"I won't. He's old enough to hear it." Ron turned back to Theo. "You were an angry little shit when you were a teen, but anyone with eyes could see through that. You were lost and hurting, and you needed to know you were loved. That's why we adopted you instead of fostering you for the next three years. Because it was as clear as day that you wanted to belong somewhere. You thought it was the army, so off you went and we didn't say anything, but Janet changes the sheets on your bed every fortnight. She hangs your stocking every December. I pay the upkeep and registration on the car you left here after high school in case you ever wanted to take it for a spin when you're back. So don't tell us this isn't your home. You might not think of it that way, but we sure as hell do."

Ron was breathing heavily when he finished, face flushed and under the bluster Theo could see the hurt pouring out of his adoptive father's blue eyes.

"I'm sorry," he managed. He turned to Janet, who was crying outright now. "I'm so sorry."

She nodded, reaching out to pat his arm. "It's okay, love."

"It's not." Theo propped his elbows on the table and clasped his hands in front of his face, resting his forehead against them. "I keep hurting people who care about me. I don't mean to, but I do. There's something wrong with me."

"There's nothing wrong with you," Janet protested.

"There is." Theo looked at her bleakly. "I've got post-traumatic stress disorder."

"So's Bob, down at the bookies," Ron shrugged. "Got it after the earthquakes. Emergency response."

"I don't think it's quite the same thing," Theo said.

"Course it is," Ron responded. "A problem is a problem, and you and Bob have the same one. Your mother and I have our problems, too. But you can deal with it. You're a good man, Theo. You can't tie your identity to an illness. As long as you don't go stupid trying to fix it with drugs or alcohol, you'll still be the same boy we met at fifteen deep down inside. A little older, a little wiser, but you're not defective. You just need to know you're loved. That's all anyone really needs in the end."

Theo searched Ron's words for a point to argue and came up short.

"I think I blew the love thing," he admitted quietly after a minute.

"Do we know him? Or her?" Janet asked softly. As a teen, Theo had thrown his bisexuality in the Millers' faces like a challenge, daring them to find a reason to forsake him. He'd never got so much as the smallest flicker of judgement to the stream of boyfriends and girlfriends he'd paraded through the house. Bob would grunt and relinquish the remote to Theo and his latest partner, in favour of retiring to his shed, and Janet would ask if the new arrival would like to stay for dinner, an invitation Theo always rejected in horror on his date's behalf.

"Unfortunately, you might. Or if not, you will soon," Theo groaned, filling them in on the situation with Ana and her title. The Avalian royal family were already staple New Zealand media gossip fodder, between Manu's sports career and both brothers having married Kiwi girls.

Janet got up at one point and reboiled the jug to make their tea, still calling questions from the kitchen as she went, and Ron pulled out his phone to search up Ana's picture, despite Theo telling him to put it away.

"Let's have a look," Janet said, carrying three mugs of tea back over to the table. "Ooh, she's a looker, Theo. You'd give me lovely grandbabies."

"She's not even talking to me right now, Mum," Theo said, trying the name on for size. He'd never used it with Janet before. He hadn't called them anything. He and Clare referred to them in conversations as 'The Millers', but when it came to in-person conversations, he'd refrained from committing to a title. He wished he'd tried it earlier though, when Janet's eyes filled with tears again and she wrapped him in a hug that smelled like Earl Grey and washing powder.

"Don't need to be talking to make a baby," she sniffled, pulling back from their embrace, and Theo cringed as Ron barked with laughter. He helped Janet with a roast chicken for dinner, and Ron with the dishes, and felt more at home in the old weatherboard three bedroom house than he ever had before, the weight of performing lifted from his shoulders. He finally felt like he was enough here. He didn't have to be surly or charming or particularly stable. The Millers had given him a home when he was a teen because they'd wanted him to know he always had a place to come home to. And, like a self-fulfilling prophecy, he'd come back to West Auckland when he had nowhere else to go, only to be welcomed with open arms.

They'd just sat down to play cribbage when Theo's phone pinged.

"Excuse me a sec," he apologised, pulling it out. It was a message from Clare.

Oliana's called a meeting. 5pm Wednesday at the palace in Avali. She wants everyone there, including you.

"Anything important, love?" Janet flicked the cards out as she dealt.

"I'm going to have to go back to Avali tomorrow," he said slowly, returning his phone to his pocket.

"Is everything okay?"

"I don't know." Maybe Ana wanted to yell at them some more. Maybe she would lock them all in one of the palace rooms with a wasps' nest. It didn't matter. If his woman wanted him there, he was going to be there.

THIRTEEN

They were gathered in an office in the palace. Six chairs had been arranged around a small desk that Ana stood behind as they filed in. Aleki, Stella, Manu, Clare and Sio quickly seated themselves, but Theo leant by the door after he closed it, leaving the last chair empty. He folded his arms across his chest, eyes flicking around the additional exits before they rested on Ana, and he released a breath he didn't know he was holding. She was exquisite. Wearing a red *puletasi*, her lush mouth painted to match, it was almost painful to look at her. To draw in the sight of the woman he loved and know he'd caused her pain almost crippled him in return. His gut churned, drawing tight, unhappiness working its way up his abdomen to gather at the base of his throat. She didn't meet his gaze, but frowned at the chair he'd left empty once the others were seated.

"Thank you for coming," she began, and his heart ached with the need to reach out and touch her. "I have visited with the king, and I would like to let you all know my plans going forward." She paused to take a deep breath and Theo noted the tense lines of her brothers' shoulders. If Ana decided to leave again there would be difficult times ahead for the royal family. Selfishly, he hoped she would.

"I have decided to stay in Avali and begin working as a member of the royal family." Disappointment sliced through his gut, a cold blade cutting through the sudden sense of relief that flooded the room as the other family members collectively exhaled.

"Don't celebrate too soon. There are conditions." Ana fixed each of her brothers with a serious gaze, the tightness around her lips signalling her stress.

"Conditions?" Sio parroted. "Like staying with your family is some kind of contract?"

Ana ignored him, and Theo let a small smirk play across his lips.

"I want to go to university." She drew a heavy breath once the words were out, as though she'd pushed them out through her chest and his heart clutched at her bravery. She was extraordinary.

Aleki nodded thoughtfully. "It would be easier if you were able to study here in Avali. Is that possible?"

"I, uh... yes." Ana managed. "Yes, that would be possible." She hesitated slightly. "I've already applied to the University of Havalei'i. It's a long shot, with classes starting early March... but are you sure?"

"Of course," Aleki shrugged. "I studied at university. Manu has an entire career in another country. We both have relationships and families outside of our work as members of the royal family. Why would it be different for you?"

"Because I'm a woman?"

"That is even more reason why you should fulfil your dreams. What an excellent example for other young Avalian women. I wouldn't worry about the registration date. Royalty has its perks. What are you planning to study?"

Ana tapped her thumb and forefinger together in a rapid staccato, the only outward sign of her nerves. "Psychology. I'm interested in learning more about why people do the things they do. Why they make the choices they do, and how their experiences affect them."

"Lovely." Aleki moved to stand, but she spoke quickly. "There's more."

"More conditions?"

"Yes."

Manu's rich laugh echoed around the office. "When you join a family, you do it with style." He grinned his big, easy grin at her. "What else do you want, *itiiti tuafafine*?"

Ana rolled her eyes at the label, which Theo's rudimentary basics translated as 'little sister', but forged ahead, her spine straighter now that her first request had gone unchallenged.

"I want to work with the government to overhaul our mental health services, focusing on the areas of grief and trauma. They are outdated, and no longer serve the development of our citizens appropriately. With more people leaving the church, they need additional outlets to work through their emotions around difficult circumstances."

Theo's breath caught in his throat, and he choked slightly. Ana's eyes jumped towards him. He almost drowned in their dark depths, but she gave nothing away, turning her head back towards her family instead.

"I don't want to be a figurehead," she added. "I want to be actively involved. Maybe not with the clients themselves, that might be a little close to home," she added. "But certainly when I finish studying, updating the policies, developing training and treatment programmes and staffing."

"All that sounds achievable," Aleki said, and from his position by the door, Theo could see the prince rolling the idea around in his head, picking it apart and looking for issues, seeing the potential and the pitfalls. A political sommelier.

"There's one more thing."

"Of course there is," her oldest brother groaned. "Let's have it, then."

"The Avalian government will offer Spire Security a contract for our cybersecurity needs going forward."

"Absolutely not." Aleki sat up straight. "We have our own security."

"And that security has failed," Ana reminded him. "I spoke to our current head of security when I returned. It took them a week to locate me once I left the island. "Tex-" she gritted out the nickname sourly, and Theo could taste her bitterness around it. Around the reminder of the pain he still suffered as a result of the moniker, and he wished he'd been able to tell her before now that nobody in this room called him that anymore. That he'd found the courage to ask for better. "-found me in less than twenty four hours. Keep the current teams in place, I'm not looking to oust anyone from their jobs, but have Spire Security implement their systems and train our staff. Everyone wins."

"Especially your boyfriend," Aleki muttered under his breath, earning himself a hard look from both his wife and Clare. Theo's gut clenched low at the words, waiting for Ana's denial, her rejection of the label, but it didn't come.

"Excuse me, but you love me, yes?" He didn't know why she was asking. All three of her brothers had told her time and time again since her return. If she struggled with believing it herself, she couldn't doubt they believed it. Still, it wasn't enough for Theo to know how they loved her. To see her settling into her role, when everything inside him screamed to scoop her up and cart her away, that the love that burned through him for her was more than any of them could imagine. He fisted his hands tightly, letting the stab of his short nails bring him back to the meeting, to the glory of his woman claiming her place in her family and the world.

"Of course."

"Well, this is the man you trusted to find me and protect me when you yourself couldn't. Any of you," she added, fixing Manu and Sio with the same raised brow. "If you love me as much as you say, you obviously consider him competent at his work. Regardless, *I* consider Spire Security to be the best at what they do. If you want me to feel like a full member of this family, my word has to count for something."

There was a beat. "Well, of course. Tex - *Theo*," Manu rushed to correct himself, as his fiancée elbowed him in the ribs "is Clare's family anyway. It would be great to have him here on a more permanent basis."

"Is that doable?" Clare pinned him with her grey eyes. "You moved to London to start the business. Is it practical to take a contract half a world away?"

Theo glanced at Ana, but she studiously ignored him.

"It can be done," he admitted. "I mean, it's the Internet. It doesn't really matter where I work from, and access isn't a problem here. I'd need to speak to Liam of course, but he could continue in London, building our network and creating further opportunities that I could manage from here. There would be some back-and-forth travel I expect, but that's not a dealbreaker. If he agrees, and there's no other reason for me to decline the contract," he said, sliding another glance at the woman who'd put this all into motion as she studied her nails with great concentration. "It wouldn't be difficult to transfer my equipment here and set up a satellite operation."

Clare smiled at him, one of the soft ones he remembered from when she was an awkward teen and it was the two of them against the world. "It would be nice to have you a bit closer," she admitted. "Auckland's only a three hour flight away."

"Okay." Stella's voice cut through the room and Theo noticed she'd been tapping away on her phone as the conversation flowed around her. "So, Theo, you'll discuss the new contract with your partner and let us know within forty-eight hours. I'll call the lawyers and get them to outline the contract once we know whether you're able to commit. Aleki?"

"*Fafine aulelei?*"

"You can call the University of Havalei'i and put in a good word to get Ana into March's student intake. Sio can put the word out with his business friends to find a suitable apartment in the city for Theo if he's going to be here for a longer period of time."

"What about me?" Manu asked, lounging back in his chair, one arm slung along the back of Clare's seat.

"You can get back to training. One grand final championship is great, but Malia wasn't there to see you win. You need to do it again this season if you're going to impress your niece."

Manu grinned. "Anything for the little one."

Stella smirked. "Softie. Okay then," she looked around the room. "Anything else? No? Lovely. We have a plan then. We'll take off and get things started." She stood and circumnavigated the desk, embracing Ana warmly. "I think you're amazing, Ana. I can't wait to see what happens next. Let us know if you need anything."

One by one the others stood and offered their embraces and platitudes. Theo pushed away from the wall and moved towards the door but he didn't get there.

"Not you, Mr Miller." Ana's voice cut through the haze in his head. "I need to speak with you privately."

Hope and logic warred in his chest, but he pushed them aside, wrestling them down so he could give Ana his full focus. She deserved that at least.

Clare gave him a sympathetic smile on her way out, and Manu clapped his shoulder. Aleki, Stella and Sio ignored him, but that was par for the course, given their loyalty to Ana. He didn't blame them at all. Then they were gone, and he was alone with Avali's princess. She moved until she was directly in front of him and the familiar rich scent of roses and coconut oil on her skin nearly dropped him to his knees. Ana dragged her eyes over him slowly, up and down, her gaze like flames licking at his flesh. As if her gaze was a tangible thing, drawing its way over the planes of his body, dangerous and desired in equal measure. When she looked up into his face he almost groaned aloud.

"Come with me," his princess commanded. "We're going for a walk."

OH GODS, *oh gods, oh gods*.

Ana was freaking out. Even as her veins sparked alight with the success of the meeting, anxiety wore a path up and down her oesophagus. She'd got him a job; the kind of contract that by all means he and Liam had been working towards. That had to count for something, right? Unless... she paused as they approached one of the large wooden doors that led to the palace grounds.

"Was that alright? The job?"

Theo's eyes were unreadable as they met hers. She thought she caught a quick flare of heat in their hazel depths, but she blinked and they were flat again. Professional. *Just the facts, ma'am.*

"It's very kind of you to consider Spire Security for such an opportunity. I'm sure Liam will be ecstatic when I pass along the offer." His words were careful, matching his neutral tone and the anxiety swirling up and down her body like an acidic maypole spilled out.

"I don't give a shit about Liam."

Theo raised a brow, and she surged on. *In for a penny...* "I mean, I do, as in he's a fellow human being and I wish him good health and a lovely life, but I don't care what he thinks about working for the Avalian government. I care about you. What do you think?"

A careful shrug. "As I said, it's very kind."

Ana almost stomped her foot. "I didn't do it to be kind."

Theo's lips twisted wryly. "I don't think you could ever be anything but kind, Ana." He pushed the door open and gestured for her to exit the palace first. She clomped out, across the wide verandah and down onto the lush grass that led to the ocean clifftop. There she stopped, the late January wind whipping her long skirt and short hair around her as she gazed out over the whitecapped waves beyond the reef. Theo came to stand beside her and they watched the water while she gathered the remaining scraps of her courage.

"I love you, Theo."

She felt him look at her then, his gaze as strong and warm as a hand cupping her face.

"You do?"

"I do." She turned to face him and his eyes shone gold with unshed tears. "Oh, sweetheart." She reached out for him and he threw himself into her arms, clutching her to him, peppering her face with kisses.

Apologies and promises spilled from his mouth in equal measure as she nuzzled into his neck and inhaled deeply. The scent of his citrus herbal soap surrounded her, and she sucked it into her lungs like a benediction, cleansing the hurt and the stains from her soul.

Eventually she pulled back a little to look up at him. She ran a finger over the beautiful hard planes of his face, the arch of his blond brow, the shell of his ear. *My love.*

"I'm sorry I didn't tell you sooner. There was a lot to process, and honestly?" she sighed, "I wasn't ready to forgive you until now."

Theo nodded solemnly, his nose grazing hers. "I know. What I did was unacceptable."

Ana sighed. "It was understandable. After all, nobody could have predicted we'd have real feelings for each other. Plus I know how insistent my brothers can be."

"Still," he replied. "I should have told you. I can't regret the time we spent together but I very much regret keeping the assignment a secret from you."

"You were right to do so," Ana admitted. "If you'd told me at the beginning... well, I'd have walked away and never looked back. We'd never have spent that time together, getting to know each other. You'd never have become one of the most important people in my world."

"Am I?"

"You are."

Theo kissed her properly then, soft and sweet. He tasted like green tea and mint, and she pressed herself flush against him, sipping at his lips until he opened them and their tongues tangled as the kiss grew more passionate. They broke apart and Ana laughed at the sight of Theo, red lipstick smeared across his mouth, grinning at her like she'd hung the moon.

"You temptress." He stole another quick kiss. "You'll have me doing unspeakable things to you in your father's garden."

Ana's smile dimmed at the reminder. "Not today. Maybe another time," she added thoughtfully. "There's a nice hedged section around the back."

Theo reached down and linked their hands as they turned back towards the palace.

"I was extremely proud of you today," he blurted as they made their way slowly across the manicured grounds.

"Thanks." Ana lifted their joined hands together and pressed a kiss against the back of his hand. "I was proud of myself. I'm finally building the life I want. You're a huge part of that."

Theo closed his eyes and exhaled. "I know it shouldn't affect me to this degree, but your life could be anything you want. The fact that you've chosen me to be a part of it... it means the world, sweetheart."

"The same for me." Ana hesitated, reluctance pulling at her, urging her away from giving up the final piece of her vulnerability. "Love, it scares me. It's not something I have a lot of experience with, not without it being used as a tool to manipulate me. My parents, the king, my brothers. Even you, at the beginning. Everyone has always told me they loved me but moved behind the scenes to keep me from knowing the truth, to steer me in certain directions. That's why it devastated me to learn that you had an ulterior motive when we met."

Theo looked pained. "I'm so sorry, sweetheart."

Ana flashed him a small smile. "I know, but the more I thought about it, the more I realised you might have been keeping your job a secret from me, but you never tried to use it against me. I wanted to stay out all night and you arranged it. I wanted to go to a protest, and you encouraged me to choose my own issue. You supported me to achieve my dreams, when discouraging me would have made your job easier. So, when you say you love me, I believe it. I believe that you don't have an agenda for wanting to be with me."

Theo groaned. "Oh, Ana. *You* are the reason I want to be with you. Just you."

"I know that now. That's why I trust you. That's why I can accept your love and offer you mine without fear."

They reached the verandah and settled in silent agreement on the steps, bodies pressed against each other, Theo's arm around her shoulders, their fingers still linked.

"Love scares me too," he admitted, quietly. "Everyone I ever loved left me, including you. I thought the only way I could protect myself was not to let anyone in, but I didn't stand a chance with you. You batted those big brown eyes at me and kissed me on Liam's mate's boat and I was lost. I was yours from that moment. When I found the list, I thought the worst. That I'd just been a stepping stone on your journey. That I was head over heels in love and you were killing time with me. I thought you'd leave me too."

Sorrow bubbled up in Ana. "I did."

"You did," he agreed. "But you were right to, and

knowing that, that I had been complicit in my own leaving made me reconsider some other elements. I went to see my parents."

"What?"

"My adoptive parents. The Millers. It turns out that they'd been waiting for me the same way I'd been waiting for you, but for a much longer time. They love me. They were just waiting for me to love them back."

"Oh, my love." She used her free hand to stroke the soft hairs on the back of his neck. "That must have been difficult."

"Letting someone in, giving up control, that's not something that comes naturally to me," he said, his thumb stroking hers. "It will take a while to get used to it. I'll probably backslide - with them and with you - but for love to persevere, for me to have the family I want, I need to trust that the people who claim to love me won't hurt me. I trust the Millers. They've never given me any reason not to, despite all my teenage angst."

"And me?" Ana's breath was in her throat.

"I trust you more than anyone. You're the reason I *can* trust, Ana. You're the light I've been looking for my whole life and I'll spend the rest of it showing you if you'll let me."

"I'd love nothing more."

Theo huffed out a laugh, pressing a quick kiss to her hair. "Even though it's not on your list?"

Ana reached into the waistband of the long skirt of her *puletasi* and pulled out a folded slip of paper. "That's the funny thing about lists," she breathed, offering it to Theo. "They can always be added to."

He shot her a quizzical look as he unfolded the page ripped from her notebook. She saw his lips move slightly as he read over the new items she'd added.

7. *Fix things with Theo*

8. *Start university*

9. *Ask Theo to marry me and have my babies.*

10. *Help Theo achieve everything on his to-do list.*

His brows shot up as he reached the final points, and his arm tightened around her. "Ana, is this... are you proposing?"

Butterflies swarmed in Ana's stomach and she squeezed his hand, bolstered by his warm, strong grip.

"Gods, no," she murmured, shrugging out of his embrace and moving forward to the edge of the verandah. "One does not propose via a to-do list." She turned back towards him and bent to one knee on the soft grass. "Now I'm proposing."

Theo's eyes were a little wild as he scanned the surrounding area. "Are you sure? What about your brothers? Your education? Hell, what about tradition?"

"Theo," Ana grasped his hand and his eyes met hers again, bright with something she couldn't put a name to. "This is what I want. You, of all people, should know by now that I will always find a way to do something I want, regardless of what other people think. You're not obligated to say yes, your job doesn't rely on your acceptance and neither does our relationship. But I want to ask, so I'm asking." She drew a deep breath and ran her thumb over his left ring finger. "Theodore Falcon Miller." She smirked at his surprised expression. "What? You're not the only one who can read a file. I love you and I want to be with you, in good times and bad. I want to hold you when you're scared and have your arms around me when I am. I want to laugh with you, cry with you, argue with you and write lists with you. Will you marry me?"

Theo looked at her for a long moment, and she swallowed back nerves that threatened to cut off her air supply as she waited for his answer. When it came, it was soft and sure, sincerity pouring out of every word.

"Oliana Rosini Maiava, nothing would make me happier."

EPILOGUE

Six Months Later

OLIANA MAIAVA WAS THRIVING.

Contentment flooded through her veins, a second skin within herself, bathing everything in a golden light. It wasn't just the champagne talking, either. She sat on the couch in one of the spare rooms of the Avalian palace, gazing out across the lawn at the large white marquee set up for Manu and Clare's wedding reception. A soft noise, and then Stella was beside her.

"It's going to be a good day," the other woman said, her voice heavy with satisfaction.

"It is," Ana agreed quietly, sharing a smile with her sister-in-law. They'd become close over the past six months, establishing a tradition of Sunday lunches together with Aleki and Theo, and Manu and Clare joining them when they were in Avali.

Manu was having the season of his life with the Auckland Knights, but despite coming up to the finals, he'd insisted on holding the wedding on the one year anniversary of his proposal to Clare. It turned out the youngest of her brothers was quite the romantic. Which meant they were gathered here in Avali on a Tuesday of all days, to accommodate the Auckland Knights' game schedule, family, workmates - Ana had already heard the staff giggling over the plethora of hot league players wandering about the complex - and the dignitaries that had missed the first Esera brother's wedding.

"Do you mind?" Ana had asked Clare that night as they sat out on the patio at Manu and Clare's house, the jagged peaks of volcanic rock and lush rainforest surroundings forming a natural protection against the paparazzi that had been stalking the couple all week in hopes of releasing the first shots of the new Royal Highnesses. Ana had been gifted her own plot of land from their mother's estate after she began royal duties and she and Theo were in the process of merrily drawing up plans for their dream island home. "All those people you don't know?"

Clare had shrugged. "It doesn't matter to me at all. I would have happily eloped. With Theo as a witness, of course," she hurried to add when Ana drew herself up to defend her fiancé's feelings. "But it matters to Manu. It's taken him so long to feel comfortable with his position in Avalian society and his position in the team. Now that he does, he wants everyone here to celebrate. I'd marry him anywhere, under any circumstances," the feisty scientist added, her face morphing into the soft smile she only wore when her husband was involved. "The only person I care about seeing tomorrow is him."

"Is he here yet?" Clare asked now, her voice coming from behind them, pulling Ana's gaze from the riot of copper curls of Stella's event planning partner Jessie darting back and forth to the marquee.

Ana turned, and gasped. Beside her Stella did the same.

"Oh gods, Clare, you look beautiful."

In keeping with Avalian wedding tradition, Clare's gown covered her shoulders but she'd made it her own. No long lace sleeves or high necks. Instead, a shimmering sheer cape style top floated over a simple strapless mermaid gown in ivory that brushed the floor. It was demure enough to keep any malicious gossip at bay and edgy enough to fit the bride perfectly. But it was her face that drew Ana's attention. Black hair pulled back in a low knot at her nape, her skin glowing and grey eyes luminous with a sweep of black liner and subtle silvery shadow. She looked happier than Ana had ever seen her, bliss rolling off her in waves. Beside her, beaming with pride was Cara, her friend from New Zealand. The leggy redhead had been in charge of hair and makeup, and she'd performed outstandingly. The first public royal wedding in Avali in thirty years was going to be a showstopper.

"Yes, I'm a ray of sunshine in an otherwise cloudy sky," Clare drawled dryly. "Is Manu here? Can you see him?"

"Oh, there he is!" Stella swivelled back towards the window. "Down by the marquee, greeting people."

The girls crowded around the window. Manu was there, flanked by Aleki, Theo and Cara's best friend, and his Auckland Knights teammate, Finn Chalmers. Cara gave a low whistle when she saw the boys. "Black, white, grey and silver. Nice colour scheme."

Clare smiled smugly. "Inspired by the scientific perspective. Not even romance is immune."

"Enough science chat." Stella rolled her eyes. "I have exactly eighteen minutes until Lani arrives with my baby and I'm back on mama duty. Let's have a toast." Moving towards the low dark coffee table, she popped open a bottle of champagne, poured two fresh glasses for Clare and Cara and topped up her own and Ana's.

"Are we toasting me?" Clare asked, accepting the tall flute.

"To love," Ana offered. "We find it in the most unexpected places sometimes -"

"The living room," Clare offered, referencing her own romance with her Manu, which had started when they were flatmates.

"The other side of the world," Ana replied.

"The back of a car," Stella sighed dreamily. "What?" she demanded when the others laughed. "We can't all be classy and take things slow like you lot."

"But wherever we find it," Ana continued, wiping a small tear of mirth from the corner of her eye, "let us thank the gods that we are smart enough to reach out and grab it with both hands. Our family has proven that when we love, we love forever. Not even death can take that from us." They paused, heads bowed in silent acknowledgement of King Tama, who had passed four months earlier, and the late Queen Tatyana who he had cherished all the days of his life. "Here is to love. Powerful, lasting, and yours. To Clare and Manu!"

"To Clare and Manu," the girls murmured in unison, and clinked their glasses together before sipping the golden liquid inside.

"That was beautiful, Ana," Stella said, wrapping an arm around her in a half-hug.

"It was," Cara agreed, a hearty swig of her champagne already gone. Ana wasn't worried though. She'd seen Cara drink Manu and Finn under the table the first night they'd all arrived on the island. Though Finn might have been a bit distracted trying not to stare down his best friend's top to keep track of his intake. "I wish I had the kind of love you guys do," the redhead added, taking another sip. "I attract freaks like a fairground. At this rate, it'll be me and Finn together at the old folks' home surrounded by a thousand cats."

"I'm sure Finn would love to grow old with you," Stella remarked lightly. She winked at Ana behind Cara's back and Ana stifled a smile. Stella had obviously seen it too.

Before Cara could respond, there was a tap at the door, and Aleki's personal assistant Lani entered, baby Malia propped on her hip. The infant was dressed in a white tutu covered with glittery silver stars and a silver bow in the short tuft of dark hair that was currently growing straight up from her head.

"*Malo, lo'u pepe*," Stella sang, reaching for her daughter.

Clare stepped into place beside Ana as Cara and Stella cooed over baby Malia.

"She's cute," the bride sighed. "Too bad we've decided not to have any."

"No?" Ana slid a glance at her sister-in-law-to-be out of the corner of her eye. Last she'd heard, Manu and Clare were still discussing the idea.

"Not for us," the other woman confirmed. "We're going to foster, maybe adopt down the track. Help give kids like Theo and I the kind of home life we wished for."

Ana's heart melted a little. "That's lovely."

"And you?"

"Oh yeah, they're definitely in the cards. God willing," Ana tacked on quickly. "Or you willing, if necessary."

"Good." Clare smiled softly, nodding as she looked towards the baby. "Theo will be the best dad."

"He will," Ana agreed, and they shared a secret smile, the smile of two women who loved the same man, albeit in very different ways.

"Clare?" Stella interjected gently. "It's time."

Clare's smile grew wider. "Hell, yeah, it is. I'll see you down there."

Ana joined the other women as they made their way down the wooden staircase of the palace to the Grand Hall. Theo stood outside the large double doors, waiting to escort Clare down the aisle. As her best man, he wore a black lavalava and a steel grey collarless shirt that Ana knew Manu had agonised over the selection of, an 'ula of frangipani and pandanus keys around his neck. A flutter of pride wormed its way from Ana's heart to between her legs at the sight of her man dressed in formal Avalian attire. He looked up and their eyes met, the flutter turning into a spark as it always did when he looked at her that way, love beaming out of his gorgeous hazel eyes.

"You look incredible," he murmured when she got closer, reaching out to snag her hand and pull her against him for a gentle kiss.

"Mmm, wait til you see Clare," she replied.

He grinned, big and bright. "She's ready?"

"She's ready," Ana confirmed.

"I'm ready, too," he whispered, nuzzling her ear. "I can't wait to marry you."

"Soon," Ana promised.

Theo lifted his head. "Very soon," he confirmed, squeezing her left hand, the hand where she wore Queen Tatyana's ruby ring, in a gentle pledge.

The official statement was that they were waiting until

Ana finished her degree to marry. Unofficially though, they were planning on stopping over in the United States on their way back from Gert and Jorge's wedding in December. Their to-do list had grown as their relationship had gone from strength-to-strength, and they'd decided to add *Elope to Las Vegas* to it a couple of months ago. Her adoptive parents would be horrified, but the more time she spent with the Esera brothers, the more she realised that the ideas she'd grown up with about how to behave didn't matter as much to her royal brothers as long as she was happy.

Nothing made her happier than the idea of running away to do something crazy with Theo; a hark back to the way they'd met.

Reaching out, she traced the edge of his tattoo, peeking up above the neckline of his shirt. The round pattern of Alexandra Palace's wide circular stained glass window in black ink. She had its twin inked onto her left hip. A memento of how they'd met, and of their journey together. The placement of the stylised rose design to the left, a sign of respect for the Avalian custom of putting a flower over your left ear to show you were taken. They'd had them done the traditional way; lying on mats in the tattooist's *fale*, the tap of handmade tools in wood and turtle shell mingling with the soft sounds of singing from their family, who gathered around the edges of the fale to encourage them.

"I'd better get back," she whispered. "Save me a dance?"

"Every dance for the rest of my life belongs to you. And so do I."

A life together. It would be their greatest adventure yet.

THE END

ACKNOWLEDGMENTS

My heartfelt thanks go out to Barbara De Leo and Hayson Manning for their ongoing feedback, encouragement and advice. I am so lucky to have their expertise to draw on. The deepest thanks to the Blenheim girls for bringing me into the fold as a newbie with a decent first chapter.

From the bottom of my heart I would like to thank the Pacific Islanders who have spent the last decade educating me in their languages and cultures, answering my questions and sharing their experiences, and Vika Mana for her work in ensuring cultural elements in this book were handled as sensitively as possible. Any mistakes are mine alone.

No book is born without a degree of suffering, and I have not suffered alone. I cannot give enough thanks to my incredible husband for the support and encouragement he has given me in this journey, even though he explicitly said 'Don't thank me, I don't need acknowledgment'. My unending appreciation also goes extends to my parents and the Disney+ app, all of whom did a little more babysitting than I'd like to admit to during this process.

ABOUT THE AUTHOR

Award-winning author Courtney Clark Michaels has been reading and writing romance since she first pilfered a novel out of her mother's bedroom at the tender age of thirteen. Courtney's passion for writing strong, independent heroines and smart, sexy men is equal only to her passions for travel, online shopping and patting other people's dogs. She is lucky enough to live in the heart of New Zealand's wine-making region with her own opposites-attract hero, a few gorgeous children and a hyperactive poochon named Kevin.

ALSO BY COURTNEY CLARK MICHAELS

PACIFIC PASSIONS

Royally Screwed

Crown Chemistry

Christmas in Paradise

Ginger Kisses

Counting Down

Storm Warning

HOT RUGBY KNIGHTS

Game Changer

Off His Game

STANDALONES

Single Dad For The Runaway Bride

Heiress Undone

A Pacific Passions story

By Courtney Clark Michaels

Previously published as *Protecting His Princess*.

www.courtneyclarkmichaels.com

Cover Illustration - Kerilyn Clarke

Ebook ISBN: 978-0-473-58031-5

Print ISBN: 978-1-0670246-9-7